LOVE ME LIKE YOU MEAN IT

LAURA BURTON

BURTON & BURCHELL LTD

First Edition

Published by: Burton & Burchell Ltd

Please contact the rights holder for translation and audio rights to this book at laura@burtonburchell.co.uk

This book is written in U.S. English

Edited by: Tochi Biko

Cover Design: Haley James PA

Love Me Like You Mean It

By Laura Burton

 Created with Vellum

CHAPTER 1

"WE ARE PLEASED TO HEAR FROM OUR NEWEST designer, Emma King, who will present to us a fresh concept shoe."

The boardroom smells like feet, but I try to ignore it. I slide my chair back and strut to the head of the table with no mishaps. So far, so good.

This is it. The opportunity I've been working for my entire career. Finally, after years and years of nagging and networking, grabbing lattes and coffees for every power-house name in the office - and sucking up to my boss - I'm here. I'm about to show my design to the board of directors at L. P

Marlowe; the number one shoe designer in Manhattan.

I try not to focus on any one person, and the sea of faces blur in front of me. Someone coughs in the back, and my hands grow clammy as I fumble with the clicker.

Relax, Emma. You've got this.

I arrived at the office early so I could check and triple check that everything was in order.

Snazzy high-tech slideshow—courtesy of techy neighbor AKA friend for life. Check.

The blinds are lowered halfway. Just enough to allow some natural light in and keep the room from resembling a dungeon, but also enough to keep sunlight from distorting my flawless presentation.

Cup of decaf coffee sitting far enough away from any electrical devices but still within reach. Check.

Nothing can go wrong.

I smooth out my Jigsaw skirt, praying the price tag doesn't fall out during the presentation, and flick my hair back with a deep breath. It's show time.

"Thank you for the introduction, Stewart. Thank you all for giving me your time today. I am excited to present to you a design you will have never seen before." I press the clicker and beam at the board of directors sitting round the conference table. "These are what I call, Schnooze shoes."

I pause, a confident smile still on show, scanning all the faces for any sign of life. My ears wait for a unified gasp of shock and awe, but I'm met with vacant stares. Just crickets.

Okay, Emma. You've prepared for this. Time for the speech.

"In a recent poll, our market researchers discovered that a whopping ninety-seven percent of New Yorkers can't wait to kick off their shoes after a long day at work. I mean, hands up if you look forward to that?"

A few shaky hands rise in the air and my spirits lift.

"Right. We also found that at least seventy-two percent of New Yorkers have hard floors in their home. And everybody hates cold feet." I wink at poor Jonesy. He invited the whole office to his wedding last year but his fiancée never showed. "Maybe if Megan had a pair of Schnooze, she wouldn't have left you at the altar. Am I right?" I laugh at my own wit with a snort, but the stares turn cold. Panic stations. I'm losing them. I need to think of something, quick. Who knows when I'll get another opportunity like this again?

"Schnooze shoes are the perfect shoe for professionals. They're fluffy on the inside but look like a normal shoe on the outside. Now, busy New Yorkers can take the comfort of their own home with them to work. So, they can schmooze at the Christmas party, and let their feet snooze at the same time."

A few people mumble, and the energy in the room shifts. I can't decide if it's a good thing or not but I take it as an opportunity to carry on.

"We had a focus group trial these shoes for two weeks and report back. As you can see on the graph here - wait sorry, not that slide - how do I go back again?"

I manically press the clicker, flipping through my slideshow, and ignore the sea of eyes recording my distress.

"This one," I say triumphantly, as the graph shows up on the screen. I wipe the sweat from my upper lip with my sleeve and do my best to carry on with my dignity intact. "As you can see here, most of our focus group reported that they enjoyed wearing the

Schnooze shoes and a whopping sixty-six percent of participants would recommend them to a friend."

A hand rises in the air, and I jump at the opportunity to answer a question.

"That number at the bottom... fourteen. Is that the sample size?" The question hangs and tightens round my neck like a noose. Drops of sweat cling to my temples and I fan myself with my cue cards. Did someone turn up the heat?

"Yes. Well, it was tricky to find enough people with the time restraints..." I trail off and wipe my upper lip again with my sleeve. To my horror, a smudge of orange makeup stains it and now I have visions of myself talking to these heavy hitters with a milk moustache.

"Emma. Don't you mean Snooze Shoes? You know they've been on the market for years." The directors talk to each other now, ignoring my presence, and my ears ring. This ship is heading for destruction, the cold look from my boss is my iceberg. But I'm not giving up.

"No, no, no. You see, these are different because Snooze shoes are just slippers. These are slippers disguised as work shoes." I have to raise my voice over the chatter now. Chairs scrape across the floor and people leave the room, shaking their heads and muttering to each other as they go.

"No, don't go. These shoes are the future. Soon, everyone in Manhattan will be wearing them, you'll see. They're going to be huge!" I can no longer hide the desperation in my voice as the last of the directors file out of the room. Then I fall quiet and stare in disbelief as the room empties and the only people left are me and my boss.

"In my office. Now," he says, his face turning gray. My stomach tightens and I think a bit of vomit just rose to my mouth. Five minutes. All those years, all those hours, all that hard work, for five measly minutes. And just like that, it's all over. My entire career is down the drain. I follow my boss with a heavy sigh and hatch a plan for the rest of the day. There's only one thing to do when your hopes and dreams get squished like a bug. Only one activity that might offer a glimmer of hope that your future won't suck as much as the present. Yes. It's time to try on wedding dresses.

CHAPTER 2

"KATIE, HAVE I EVER TOLD YOU THAT YOU ARE the best friend anyone could have?" I ask, looking at my roommate with stars in my eyes. The right corner of her mouth lifts, but she's too modest to reply. Instead, she tucks blonde hair behind an ear and disappears behind me, tugging on the dress to work the zipper.

Not just any dress. *My* dress. At least, it will be mine when Mr. Right shows up on my door on bended knee brandishing a diamond ring. Sure, I'd have to sell my apartment - and probably a kidney - to pay for it, but Vera Wang is worth it.

"So, I take it the presentation didn't go as you planned?" Katie asks, her fingernails graze the back of my neck as she works the loops. I laugh derisively at the question.

"Oh, it went to plan. I mean, apart from a little technical hiccup, I did everything just like we rehearsed."

"Then I don't get it. Is this a celebratory fitting?" Katie reappears and eyes me with suspicion.

She manages the most expensive bridal store on Fifth Avenue. Noelle's. One perk of being her best friend is that I get to come in and try on dresses whenever I want. Besides, people see me trying on these outrageously expensive gowns through the window, which is good advertising, right? I swear, trying on a designer wedding dress works better than Xanax. It's arguably just as addictive, though.

There's something about standing on the cushioned stool, surrounded by floor mirrors and dazzling lights, swishing the big skirt side to side, that just makes me all warm and fuzzy inside.

I am Emma King.

Talented designer, delightful conversation-alist and drop-dead gorgeous female any man would be lucky to have.

At least, that's who I am when I'm in this dress.

It fits snug on my waist and forces me into the perfect posture. I feel regal, poised, elegant. It gives me the courage to tell the truth.

"They hated my design," I blurt, my brain settling back on the very reason I'm here. My eyes dart to the box in the corner of the room, the entire contents of my desk sitting inside. "Then my boss fired me."

The words sting. They slide off my tongue like I'm spitting blades and it makes my eyes water. Katie gasps, her slender hand flies to her open mouth and her wide eyes turn glassy.

"The Schnooze shoes? I think they're genius. Look, I'm wearing them now." She turns and bends a knee, lifting her right foot in the air with grace.

"So, that's where my prototypes disappeared to."

Katie lowers her foot again and her face turns crimson.

"I can't believe they fired you because they didn't like your design," she said, folding her arms and looking up at me like she doesn't believe me.

But why would I lie about this?

"Steven didn't fire me because he didn't like the design," I explain. "He fired me because he stuck his neck on the line to give me that pitch. In his words, I was an 'embarrassment to the company.' To be fair to him, I told him to fire me if the pitch didn't go well."

Katie gawps at me like a fish, her eyes bulging as she gasps.

"You're kidding."

I shrug haphazardly, and almost wobble off the stool, my sophistication is dropping by the second.

"I was so confident the board would love my design, I placed a bet with Steven."

Katie throws her head in her hands with a groan. I need not say any more. This is not the first time a bet has got me into trouble. In fact, if I'm going to place a wager, I should bet on myself losing the bet. If I'd done that on all the bets I've ever placed, I'd be a millionaire by now.

Slight exaggeration, maybe. But I'd be filthy rich.

The china bell hanging over the door rings and we stop our conversation to look up.

I have one of those delayed reactions as

my brain recognizes one of the women who has just entered the boutique among an entourage of ladies. Problem is, I can't place her.

My boss' ex-girlfriend Hannah? No, she didn't have blonde hair. Miss yoga pants from apartment 50a? No, she's too tall. I suck in the air around me and hold my breath as my brain scans through hundreds of headshots and memories. Then the dots add up and the picture becomes all-too clear, setting my blood into an ice-freeze.

"Oh, please, no," I whisper.

I need to get out of here. Pronto.

The skinny blonde has had her lips done, giving her a permanent pout. I don't think she's seen me yet. At least, her glittering eyes do not fly in my direction. If I can just dash into one of the changing rooms without being seen...

"Emma?"

I've bunched up the skirt of my dress so high I can no longer see anything. A twitter of hushed voices surrounds me and my heart sinks. They found me.

Well, it's not very hard. I'm standing dead center in the middle of a bridal boutique, wearing the biggest dress in the world.

"Emma King, is that you?"

I lower the skirts in defeat and put on my best smile.

"Shelly Bones! Fancy seeing you here," I say, my New Yorker accent fading and sounding oddly posh. British, perhaps?

Shelly is my high school frenemy. We were friends - kinda. We always ended up liking the same guys, and the run up to prom escalated to a full-blown war as we both wanted to be prom queen. Neither of us got it, of course. Who could compete with Harper Fox, the six-foot blonde with the supermodel mom?

"It is you!" Shelly cries, her voice far too high to sound convincingly delighted. She's just a mortified as I am. I can see it in her eyes. "How long has it been?"

Since the last time we were in the same room?

Not long enough.

Last time we spoke, it was graduation. I threw my shoe at her head when I found her kissing my boyfriend under the bleachers.

"So, you're getting married! Congratula-tions. Do I know the lucky guy?" she asks. Her posse leans in and eyeballs me as if they're a rally of reporters and I'm at a press conference. Katie stands to the side, staring at us all like she's watching a talk show. Give us five minutes and she'll be screaming, "Hit her with the chair!"

Or not. Katie is too sweet for that.

"The guy?" I say, biting my tongue as I step down.

"Your fiancé, silly," Shelly says with a giggle that sends a chill down my spine.

"Oh. No, no," I say, playing it cool. "You know; I feel like even I don't know who he is."

Nervous laughter fills the room as Katie catches onto the situation, and finally jumps into action.

"Can I get you ladies a drink?"

She disappears out back while I hover on the spot, wondering whether to make a break for the exit, or run for the changing room and lock myself in until they leave. I picture myself running around central New York in a huge wedding dress like a fairy tale character.

"Well, Frederick and I met in Africa," Shelly says, clearly undeterred by my inner turmoil. "He was building new schoolhouses, while I was running the vaccination program."

I am impressed with my restraint. My eyes remain on Shelly instead of rising to the ceiling. I fix a smile on my face too.

"Africa? Wow."

Shelly thrusts a phone into my face and her claw-like nail swipes through endless photos. Frederick is not at all like the picture I had constructed in my mind. He's tall and athletic. Tanned. He's kissing Shelly in almost every photograph. I try not to heave.

"We've been together for five years now," Shelly continues, her sickly-sweet voice making my stomach churn with each syllable. "Last year, he took me to Venice and popped the question during a gondola ride at sunset."

Shelly and her girls break out in one collective sigh.

"How romantic," I say through gritted teeth. Thankfully, the shuffling noise behind me announces Katie's return. She appears with stemmed glasses on a silver platter and I manage to stop myself from snatching one.

"So, come on. I'm dying to know about you. Where did you meet this mystery man? Have you booked a venue yet?"

I gulp my drink to build courage and buy some time. I need to just come out with it and tell the truth. There is no guy. There never was a guy. I have spent the last decade fighting my way up the career ladder only to get fired at the end of it.

So now I'm guy-less and jobless.

But this is Shelly, who's been doing humanitarian work in Africa. She probably joined the Peace Corps too. Not only that, she's engaged to some equally charitable and sexy bachelor who wants to sweep her off her feet in every European country there is.

I take another swig and make the decision to tell the lies of all lies. Just this once.

"We're having a small ceremony at the Plaza hotel."

A sea of wide eyes stare back at me - Katie's the widest of all. It only spurs me on. "He's quite the romantic, actually. We've got a string quartet and a harpist for the wedding march. Perrier Francé is catering."

"Perrier. The Perrier Francé?" Shelly says in a revered tone. I had read an article about his restaurant in the city earning 5 Michelin stars. Who knows if he even caters for weddings? But creating this elaborate lie is the most fun I've had in months.

I ramble on about caviar and that instead of wedding gifts, we're asking for donations for a charity for the Children's Hospital.

Shelly asks about my fictional fiancé again and this time I don't hold back, my imagination doing overtime.

He's the sexiest bachelor in Manhattan. So stinking rich, he focuses his energy on helping people, and he's totally devoted to me. We met in London on a rainy day. He offered me his umbrella to keep me from getting soaked and it was definitely love at first sight.

"He's booked our honeymoon in Bora Bora. We're going to plant trees there and rescue pandas."

"There's pandas in Bora Bora?" Katie asks with her face twisting. I finish my drink.

"Yes, there's pandas in Bora Bora," I say with a laugh, as if she's the most foolish person on the planet to even ask the question. "They're extinct though, it's tragic really. That's why we want to help."

A stunned silence follows, and I cough as the back of my throat burns.

"What did you put in this, vodka?" I say with a giggle, raising my empty glass.

Katie's brows lift. "It's just orange juice."

I glance at the women; their glasses are frozen in mid-air and they're all staring at me like I've just declared the Earth is flat.

"Right. It's got a bit of a kick," I say in a raspy voice, handing her the glass.

"When are you getting married?" Shelly asks, then takes a sip of her untouched drink.

"April eleventh," I blurt. It's the first date that springs to mind. Shelly splutters and gags as the ladies gasp and twitter to each other with excitement. It's not the reaction I expect, maybe her orange juice is strong too.

"I'm getting married on April eleventh too! What a coincidence."

I mirror her excited face and we both squeal, I'm 100% sure we're both faking it now.

"Well, I guess you can't make it to my wedding then," I say with a shrug.

A wave of giggles follows, and I take the opportunity to give Katie a pointed look.

"Wow, is that the time? We need to get you out of this dress, don't you have a date?" she says, tugging on my elbow. I tap my forehead, exaggerating my movements as I edge away.

"Yes. Time ran away with me. It was great to see you again, Shelly. Good luck with the wedding!"

"You too, Emma. So thrilled we both got our happy endings."

The words sit on my chest like an anvil as I dash into the changing room and hide.

CHAPTER 3

How is it possible for a little white lie to spiral so much? I've no idea where the pandas in Bora Bora came from. I shake my head with a cringe as I fumble with the keys in my door.

At least I can hide in my apartment and pretend that I'd been asleep all day and none of these crazy events ever happened. The door clicks and swings open, and I stare open-mouthed at the helium balloons filling my whole apartment.

"Surprise! Happy Birthday Emma."

My heart plummets to the pit of my stomach and a sickly sense of nausea rises to my chest as I scan the faces in my apartment.

A picture of my own face grins at me from the world's largest cake, as it's thrust under my nose. The candles illuminate the soft grey eyes of my techy neighbor, who seems to read me like a book. His expression transforms from excitement to sheer horror. It's as if he just found out the exact day and time of his own death. Which will be soon, if I find out he planned this party.

I'm always saying I love surprises and I may have had one too many late-night rants to my friends about how only people on TV get surprise birthday parties.

But today? I just want to hide.

"Do you want me to get rid of them?" he whispers. The room is still clapping; somebody blows a horn.

"If you want to live," I reply acidly. I don't mean to sound cold, and my stomach pangs at the hurt in his eyes. But it's been a day. The last thing I need now is the responsibility of pretending I'm absolutely fine while I entertain a room full of people all evening.

"There's our baby girl; thirty already. Where have the years gone?"

I stiffen at the sound of my mother's voice

and swivel on the spot, plastering my best smile on my face.

Who called my parents?

"Mom. Dad. It's great to see you." They pull me in for a hug and the familiar scent of home baked cookies floods my senses. Mom is always baking. The smell unknots my stomach for a moment and the sudden urge to break into tears crashes over me like a tidal wave.

"How did the pitch go?" Dad asks. I can't look him in the eye. Seeing his happy expression turn into disappointment will be too much for me to keep the emotions at bay.

Katie walks in through the open doorway and her mouth hangs open in shock as her eyes take in the scene.

She's just as surprised as I am.

"Aiden, can I talk to you for a second?" She tugs on the elbow of my techy neighbor, her face colorless and eyes like saucers. I turn my attention back to my mother, who is speaking at full speed.

"I know you didn't want us to make a fuss this year, but this is a big birthday, and when Aiden called, we thought…"

Aiden. AKA soon-to-be dead techy neighbor.

21

I go to shoot him a look, but he and Katie are gone.

"It's great to see you have so many friends," Dad says, looking at the room full of people. I resist the urge to laugh. These are not my friends. They're barely acquaintances who live in the building. Though I'm surprised everyone has decided to show up. Even Miss. Yoga Pants. Aiden probably bribed them all to come.

I open my mouth to say something, but nothing comes out. The words bubble in the back of my throat and my eyes start to burn.

"Is everything alright?" My mother's senses are on point. Her hazel eyes reflect my own, and narrow as they take in my appearance. She probably noticed the chocolate stain on my shirt—from the pity party I had at the donut café on the way home.

Why didn't I put on waterproof mascara today? I can sense the big drops of tears threatening to fall, sending a trail of black down my cheeks at any moment.

"I'm fine," I say in a high-pitched voice. My throat is so tight; I sound like a strangled cat. But before she can press me further, the most ear-splitting alarm breaks our conversation.

"Oh dear, that's the fire drill. We better get out of here," Aiden announces from the doorway. He's a terrible liar. His forehead is red and shiny, and his eyes look far too shifty to look convincing.

But nobody questions him. Within seconds, the apartment is emptied as a stampede of strangers race for the door.

Everyone but my parents however, who do not move but frown at Aiden instead.

"That's not the fire drill," my dad says frankly. He's not going to be fooled, not with him being a fire fighter and all. Aiden's face flushes red as he pulls out his smart phone. With a tap, the squealing stops.

"I've made a grave error in judgment," Aiden says in his deep, gravelly voice. Katie throws the door shut and bolts it, just in case anyone thinks about trying to come back in.

My mom throws her hands up in exasperation. "Can somebody please tell me what's going on here?" I exchange looks with Katie, who gives me the look. The one that says are-you-going-to-tell-them-or-am-I? With a deep breath, I turn to my parents.

"It was a disaster. They hated my design, and I got fired." The words tumble out of me so fast it throws me off balance and the next thing I know, my face is buried in my dad's shoulder. My mom wraps her arms around me, and it takes every ounce of my resolve not to let my knees buckle and break down in tears.

So much for turning thirty. I'm terrible at adulting.

My parents pat my back and shush me like I'm a three-year-old who has just scraped her knee in the playground.

"We're so sorry baby, we all know how much this job meant to you," my mom says soothingly as she strokes my hair. I can't remember the last time she's done that. I get a handle on my emotions and step back with a sniff. Aiden and Katie stand frozen by the front door, looking equally awkward.

A weighted silence follows as I avoid their awkward stares. Breaking down to my parents, in front of my friends, on my birthday, is a new low for me. But the truth is out there, and the weight on my chest lifts just enough for me to catch my breath.

Just then, a phone vibrates. I look up and

catch Katie glancing at her screen. Her eyes nearly pop out of their sockets before she stuffs it back in her pocket.

"Do you want to come home with us? I've got your room all set whenever you're ready."

My mom would love that. She's been hoping and praying that my life in the city wouldn't work out so I can return home with my tail between my legs.

"Well baby, it's their loss. I for one, think the Snooze shoes are a fantastic concept."

"It's Schnooze, dad, but thanks," I say glumly.

A phone pings. This time it's Aiden's turn to look at his screen and react. His eyes land on me and he looks at me like he's staring at a ghost.

"You know what, I'm not feeling too great, actually," I say, rubbing my aching stomach. Already a headache is starting to brew, and I know that if we keep talking, I'll lose my battle and end up making a fool of myself. I can bottle up my emotions for so long before they spill out uncontrollably.

"You do feel warm," my mom says thoughtfully as she presses the back of her hand against my clammy forehead. "You want me to make you some soup?"

I catch a glimpse of Katie and Aiden whispering to each other in my peripheral vision. They're probably thinking this is pathetic.

"No, if you don't mind. I just want to crawl into bed. I'll call you tomorrow, okay?" I pretend to yawn to emphasize my point and my parents pull me in for another squeeze.

A tear leaks out of my eye, but I furiously wipe it away before we break apart.

"Well, I'm sorry this didn't turn out the way you hoped. And I'm so sorry about your birthday honey. We'll celebrate when you're feeling better."

Aiden opens the door and we all wave and say our goodbyes as they walk out. Then Katie closes it again and the three of us breathe.

Another ping. This time Aiden and Katie exchange looks, and I frown at them.

"What on earth is going on with you two?" I rest my hands on my hips. "And which one of you thought it would be a good idea to throw me a surprise party?"

Aiden and Katie point to each other. I roll my eyes. Then a phone vibrates again. Katie's eyes fly to her screen and widen with horror.

"Um. Emma…"

The shocked whisper gives me chills. What can it possibly be now? I don't say anything but look from Aiden to Katie, waiting for the revelation.

"Remember the friend you saw at the boutique?" Katie says. I turn numb.

"Yeah…"

My own phone vibrates, I rummage in my bag and pull it out.

126 notifications.

My horrified gaze lands on Katie as she stares back.

"No. This isn't happening," I whisper.

CHAPTER 4

"I GUESS I SHOULD SAY CONGRATULATIONS?"

Aiden Daniels is not a funny guy. And yet, he likes to think he is hilarious. On his thirtieth birthday, for example, he tried doing stand-up comedy at Sam's club, one of the nicest clubs in the city.

He was the only act to get booed off the stage. Now I want to boo at him.

"I can't believe this," I say, holding my head in my hands. Katie guides me to the couch and Aiden brings over a glass of water. He passes it to me and the two of them talk in hushed tones, acting like I'm not even there.

"It's not funny Aiden, everyone's sending her messages about it."

"It's a good thing her parents aren't on social media."

I'm still numb. In fact, I think I'm having an out-of-body experience and this whole charade is happening to someone else. I look down at my phone again as it pings.

"Congratulations to my old friend, Emma King, on her engagement. Enjoy the plaza and a lifetime of happiness - Shelly Bones."

Curse you, social media. What happened to the good old days, when you could tell a white lie about being engaged and no one else would find out?

Why must we now have smartphones with apps that spread the white lie and turn it into a big black entanglement of fake news? Thankfully, I didn't give her my fiancé's name, so at least it's only mine that's tagged.

Except for Perrier Francé, who she's been able to tag on Instagram in one of her other posts.

"Why does this person think you're getting married?" Aiden asks, looking at me with a mixture of amusement and incredulity. I throw my head in my hands again and groan as Katie tells the story.

"She bumped into an old school friend at

Noelle's and just came out with this elaborate story about her amazing fiancé and the extravagant upcoming wedding."

"It wasn't just an old school friend," I say. "It was Shelly. She was going on and on about her perfect life, volunteering in Africa with her rich boyfriend who looks like an action figure."

"Is this the same Shelly your boyfriend cheated on you with?" Aiden asks, looking thoughtful.

And just like that, my annoyance washes away and Aiden is my best friend again. He says no more, but the look in his eyes is all the validation I need.

He gets it.

"Exactly," I say.

Aiden drapes his arm around my shoulder, and I spot Katie tapping away at her phone with vicious concentration. Her tongue is sticking out.

"What are you doing?" I ask her. My phone vibrates again, so I turn it off.

"I'm sending Shelly a private message, telling her to put the post down."

"What!" I shriek, sitting upright. Aiden's

arm drops behind me and he grumbles, but I ignore him.

"Don't do that. If Shelly finds out it was all a lie, she'll never let me live it down."

Katie drags a hand over her face with a sigh.

"But Emma… have you seen how many followers Shelly has? You're blowing up on social media. Everyone's asking who the fiancé is."

"It's best if you tell the truth," Aiden says with a reassuring nod, but the action does nothing to reassure me. Haven't I done enough truth telling today? Owning up to my parents about losing my job took all of the courage I had left.

"I can't," I say in a weak voice. The words sound lame and the unimpressed stares from my friends do not help.

"What do you expect me to do? Write up a post and say, 'Hey, funny story… I got fired from my job today, tried on wedding dresses and bumped into a friend who thought I was getting married… so I sort of came up with a few white lies and now the world thinks Perrier Francé is baking me a cake.' Yeah, like that's happening."

"Why not? I'm sure you're not the only person to have a fake fiancé," Katie says with a shrug; as if I lied about something superficial like my weight, or how many donuts I ate today.

"Well, you have to do something. News travels fast and when your parents find out…"

Oh, no. My parents.

Just the thought of them finding out about this sends chills down my spine. My mom will pack up my things and move me back home in an instant. My dad will be so ashamed.

Then I'll spend the rest of my days living at my parents' house, not trusted to embark out into the world on my own ever again. Now, I really do feel sick.

"You know what, it's getting late. I'm going to just go to bed and figure it out in the morning with a fresh head." I get up and edge away, grinning sheepishly at the incredulous faces of my best friends.

"It's only nine-thirty," Katie says, glancing at her watch. Aiden motions to follow me but I raise a hand, stopping him in his tracks.

"Emma, you can't hide from this. The longer you leave it, the harder it's going to be to come clean," he says firmly. He's got his ultra-serious face on now. It's the same expression he uses whenever he takes a work call.

"Oh yes I can," I argue. "My phone is off and I'm going to bed."

Before anyone can argue, I make a dash for the hall and burst into my room. The door slams behind me and I press my back up against it, listening to the thumping of my heartbeat.

Thanks to Shelly-miss-big-mouth, the whole world of social media thinks I'm getting married. But that'll have to wait until I've had some Tylenol and an early night. Perhaps, if I'm really lucky, I'll wake up and find that this day was all a bad dream, and I'll be getting ready for the big pitch.

Either that, or I'll be hunting for a new job.

And possibly a new identity too.

CHAPTER 5

I LOVE NEW YORK. WAKING UP TO THE rattling of windows as honking taxi cabs rush by reminds me I'm in the center of all the action. This city never sleeps, and the possibilities here are endless.

As an attractive bachelorette with a Masters in Fashion and a brain for business, I was born to live in the city.

But now, I might have to pack up and move to a place where no one knows me.

Where is Reykjavik?

Even though I've slept for twelve straight hours, my mind is no clearer than it was last night. I trudge into the living area, glancing at Katie's bedroom door as I pass, hoping it doesn't fly open. My heart sinks at the sight of my office belongings sitting in their cardboard box in a corner of the room.

Nope, it was not some vivid nightmare. I've lost my job and had the worst birthday surprise ever; hundreds of messages congratulating me on my - fake - engagement.

But today is a new day and I'm a smart gal. I can totally figure this out. All I need to do is get a new job and tell the world the engagement was just a big misunderstanding. Someday, I'll look back on this whole charade and laugh.

Right? Right?!

My thoughts turn to Aiden, he stayed up all night perfecting my presentation for me, then threw a surprise party to make my thirtieth birthday special. I repaid him by going crazy, sending everyone home and running to my room! I owe him an apology. And cake. Thankfully, there is a giant chocolate cake with my face on it. Literally.

And so, a plan is made.

I sing to myself in the shower, completely burying my head in the sand over the fact that I am now a thirty-year-old woman with a job hunt ahead of me. Then I pick a pair of jeans and attempt to pull them over my swollen hips, jumping up and down to aid the process.

Too many donuts, Emma. When will you learn?

The more sensible part of my brain suggests that I need to go shopping for new clothes, instead of reprimanding myself for over-indulging. Then I remember that my income has stopped, and I can't.

It doesn't take me long to style my hair and get ready. I wrap up the biggest slice of cake known to man and plaster my most endearing smile on my face as I leave the apartment and walk across the hall. My stomach does flips as I knock and wait.

The door swings open, and Aiden stands in the doorway, dripping wet and only wearing a towel. This is not the first time he's answered the door like this, but today the sight of him sends a flush of heat to my cheeks.

"Morning Aiden," I say, trying to sound chipper but my voice wobbles. "I know I was a jerk yesterday. I just wanted to swing by and say sorry."

Aiden's eyes lower to the cake in my hands and his dark brows rise.

"Is that for me?" he asks. I nod like an overly excited puppy.

"It's a peace-offering."

"It's your forehead," Aiden says with a smirk.

"Well, I thought it would be weird to bring you a cake of my eyes staring at you, and totally inappropriate to eat my mouth. Nobody wants to bite into ears. Considering you printed my face on the entire cake, I had limited options."

Aiden gives me the look. The one where he's thinking I'm crazy, but he's too sweet to say it aloud.

"You really put a lot of thought into this, didn't you?" he says, humored. My heart leaps.

"Does this mean you're not mad at me anymore?" I ask, hopeful. Aiden chuckles as he takes the cake off my hands and shakes his head. Drops of water fly from his hair and land on my face. I don't even bother trying to wipe them off as they start to make their way down my cheeks.

"Come on. Why would I be mad at you? I'm mad at the guy who fired you. He's the real jerk, not you. And the girl with the big mouth you bumped into at Noelle's, I'm mad at her too. I mean, who blurts out news like that all over social media? It's your news to share."

This here is why we're best friends. I'm pretty sure he's the sweetest guy in the world. I'd date him in a heartbeat if I wasn't so bothered about ruining our friendship.

If we did go there - and looking at his beautifully sculpted torso, glistening at me, I'm reminded of how much a part of me really wants to - there would be no going back. If things fall apart in the love department, can we really go back to being just friends? No.

Before I can reply, my back pocket vibrates. I frown and pull my phone out, bracing myself to see what damage Shelly has done now. When I see my mom's face on the screen, I breathe a sigh of relief.

"Hi mom, listen, I'm sorry about last night-

"Why didn't you just tell us the truth?" My mom interrupts me, and the question throws me off guard. What truth?

"Your aunt Bev just called. She was having her hair done by Lacy this morning, and you know she cleans for Mr. and Mrs. Bones, right?"

My heart stops and I stare at the confused face of my half-naked neighbor who has decided that now is the perfect time to tuck into my cake.

How can news travel that fast?

Aiden was right. I should have cleared everything up last night.

"Oh no," I whisper. Aiden stops chewing and looks at me with puzzlement. But my mom isn't finished.

"It is just like you to pull something like this. Who is he? Were you going to even invite us to the wedding? Oh, no. You're not doing a ceremony at the registry office, are you?"

I recoil back. Her questions hit me square between the eyes, and I swear I see baby cherubs flying around my head. This isn't happening. I swallow and muster the courage to set her straight, but before I can utter a syllable, my mom says the last thing I expect to come out of her mouth.

"Forget it. Either way, your dad and I are thrilled."

I almost drop the phone. Thrilled?

"You-you are?" I stutter, eyeing Aiden

warily, wishing he could swoop in and save me from this awkward conversation.

"Your dad and I want to have you over for dinner. We have so much to catch up on."

My stomach twists into knots and I look up at the ceiling, as if hoping there might be post-it notes up there, with something safe and intelligent to say.

"Sure," I say in a strangled voice. But my mom is too happy to notice.

"Great. I'll make your favorite."

I end the call and stand frozen, staring at Aiden as he demolishes my cake. He swallows and his expression turns thoughtful.

"Penny for your thoughts?"

The question snaps me out of my horrified daze, and I step back. "My parents want me to come over for dinner... to talk about the wedding."

"What wedding?" Aiden asks. I cock a brow at him, and his mouth turns to the shape of an o. "I hate to say, 'I told you so,' but..."

I clutch my face in a vain attempt to stop my head from spinning. Nausea rises from the pit of my stomach again.

"She sounded so happy. I can't bear to let them down. Again."

"You're going to tell them the truth though, right?" Aiden asks, putting the cake down and leaning against the doorframe. The morning light ripples across his muscles. When he's wearing his polo shirt, no one would ever guess he has a body sculpted by Leonardo DaVinci hiding underneath. I become aware that I've been staring at his pectorals and I look up quickly, only to meet his doe eyes with burning cheeks.

"Of course, I am," I blurt. Trying to force my brain back on track. Aiden nods and his shoulders sag with relief.

"Well, good luck and let me know how it goes…" he steps back and starts to close the door, but I dash forward and slam my palm on it with a bang.

"Will you come with me?" I bat my lashes at him with my best impression of puppy dog eyes. Aiden looks startled for a moment, but he recovers quickly.

"What do you need me for?"

"Moral support? My getaway driver when I drop the bombshell? Please. I need a friend."

"What about Katie?" Aiden asks, crossing his arms.

"She's going out with Colin tonight. Please do this for me. I'll walk your dog."

"I don't have a dog,"

"Right. I'll take your shirts to the dry cleaner. I'll set you up on a blind date. I'll give you a kidney!"

Aiden drops his hands and chuckles.

"How about you come with me to see a movie next week, I hate going alone?"

I hold out my hand with a grin and he shakes it. "Deal. You're the best friend ever, you know that, right?" I say squeezing his bicep. Aiden chuckles again, his fake serious expression dissolving.

"Yeah. I know. Just don't forget it."

CHAPTER 6

AIDEN PULLS UP OUTSIDE MY PARENTS'
townhouse and I suck in the air between my
teeth. The car ride out of the city was too fast
for my comfort. I'm not ready for this.

How do I face the excited faces of my
parents and give them the crushing news? My
stomach flips as we get out of the car, and I
walk round to join Aiden, clinging onto his
arm like he's my security blanket.

"Be brave. You can do this." He senses my
nerves and strokes my hair as we walk up the
brick steps to the house. I nod, unable to open
my mouth and raise my knuckles to the door,
but before I can knock, it flies open.

"I knew it!" My mom's voice is triumphant

as her eyes take in the sight of Aiden and I, standing arm in arm.

"George, I was right. It is Aiden."

My brain doesn't compute what she's saying, but Aiden looks stunned.

"Well, don't just stand there. Come on in," my mom says, stepping aside. I let go of Aiden's arm and stagger into the hall, still reeling. What's happening?

"Don't you two look adorable together!" My mom pulls Aiden in for a hug. He pats her back and opens his mouth, but no sound comes out.

"So, you're marrying my favorite daughter?" My dad walks in, his eyes set on a paralyzed Aiden. He slaps Aiden's shoulder and I swallow the uncomfortable lump in the back of my throat.

"We have amazing news," my mom announces, waving her hands to add emphasis to her words. My heart is already racing. I dread to think what fresh revelations are coming. "We were told you were asking for donations to the Children's Hospital instead of gifts. Well, your dad and I made some calls. And…" She makes a drum roll on her legs. "We've already raised twenty-five thousand dollars for the hospital. Isn't that amazing?"

Aiden and I glance at each other before we both make fake noises of delight.

"How did you know about the donations?" I ask with gritted teeth. My mom and dad lead us into the dining room, both talking at top speed.

Turns out, big-mouth-Shelly had shared all the details with her parents. Who, it seems, are still in contact with my folks? Go figure. In their generation, even without social media, news travels like wildfire.

"Take a seat at the table. George, will you get some bubbly from the cellar? I'll get the casserole out of the oven." My mom and dad leave the room and I have a mini breakdown to Aiden.

"Twenty-five thousand dollars, what are we going to do?"

Aiden scratches the back of his neck as a flush of color floods his face.

"They think I'm the groom," he says in a hollow voice. I wince. In hindsight, bringing Aiden for moral support may have just made this whole situation a lot more difficult to explain. I can see why my parents think we're engaged. Why else can Aiden be here? They don't know about my plan to shatter all their hopes and dreams of their daughter getting married at the Plaza hotel. I look at him with apologetic eyes.

"I'm so sorry, but can we please just play along until I think of something?" I whisper. Aiden hums with his brows furrowed.

He is allergic to lying. This goes against every code in his book. But this is an emergency. I need time to think. How can I say the wedding is a hoax after some hospital I made up, that actually turns out to be real, has got a big chunk of cash?

"Think of the children, Aiden," I say. My eyes tear up as I look at him. I rest a hand on his arm and his muscles tense under my touch. After a moment, he gives me a fraction of a nod and my heart leaps.

This guy. I swear, he deserves an award. I make a mental note to buy him the best Christmas present ever. Right after I get another job, of course.

Dinner is not as awkward as I expect it to be, now that Aiden is my fictional fiancé and my parents are still living under the illusion that I'm finally getting my happy ever after. In their eyes, I don't even need a job. Soon I'll be Mrs. Daniels, a stay at home mom of two kids. A boy and a girl. We'll be having family dinners at my parents every Sunday and the Schnooze shoes will just be one of the funny stories we tell the kids at bedtime.

The idea is only mildly nauseating, which surprises me. Aiden holds my hand as we talk over coffee. I wonder if it's to comfort himself or me. My dad then invites him into the garden for a talk and my blood turns cold. He's going to give him the talk. I can sense it.

"Dinner was amazing mom, you do make the best chicken casserole," I say, helping her load the dishwasher. I squint as I try to catch a glimpse of Aiden and my dad through the dark windows. My efforts are fruitless. I look back at my mom and she has her arms folded. There's a look on her face.

"Why didn't you tell us you were getting married to Aiden?"

I bite my lip and mess with the buttons on the dishwasher to buy myself some time. I hate lying too, and my brain silently rewrites the scene in the bridal boutique.

"Oh, hey Shelly. I'm just having a bad day so I'm trying on some wedding dresses to cheer myself up. I'm not actually getting married."

The other women snigger to each other, one of them snorts. Shelly beams at me with a smug half smile on her face.

"How pathetic."

Then they all throw their heads back and cackle like witches.

"Why do you say it like that?" I blurt. Back in the present. "You sound like Aiden isn't a surprise choice?"

My mom rests a hand on my shoulder and cocks her head to the side.

"Oh, baby girl. I'm your mom, I've seen the way he looks at you. I know you've had a crush on him for years."

The way he looks at me. Part of me wants to interrogate her further. How exactly does he look at me? Does she think we'd make a good couple?

Then I remember we're supposed to be engaged and those questions will definitely raise suspicion.

"Is it that obvious?" I ask. Here I am thinking I can lie to my mom about getting married, when she knows I like Aiden even though I've always tried to hide it.

"You can't get anything past me," my mom says with a smirk. I want to laugh at how wrong she is, but the giggle catches in my throat and I feel sick.

"Now come on, let's leave the rest of those dishes and have a chat. I'm not going to take no for an answer. Let me take you cake tasting this weekend too."

I glance over my shoulder at the dark window with a twinge of guilt, then follow my mom out of the kitchen. Oh, what a tangled web we weave, and now I've roped Aiden into it too.

I'm going to have to think of something really epic to get out of this bind.

CHAPTER 7

Even though we get caught in traffic on the bridge, Aiden remains silent for the entire car ride home. I swear I can hear his teeth grinding and his thoughts churning. He's obviously mulling over what happened at my parents' house.

"How did it go?" Katie asks as I enter the apartment. Aiden barely even said goodnight before he disappeared behind his door. I wonder if he'll ever talk to me again.

I slump onto the couch and pull a blanket over me as Katie switches off the TV to take a good look at my sorry state.

"You didn't tell them, did you?" she asks, doing little to hide the disappointment in her voice. I shake my head, then throw my face into my hands.

"They think I'm marrying Aiden," I moan into my fingers. "It's such a mess."

Katie nudges a mug of hot cocoa into my hands and I look up at her.

"I bet that was awkward," she says with a smirk. "What did Aiden tell them?"

My lack of response sends her brows rising to her hairline.

"He went along with it?"

I tell her every tiny detail of the evening, especially about the huge donations my parents have raised. When I finish, she whistles and takes a thoughtful sip of her own drink.

"Wow. He really has it bad for you."

I nearly choke on my drink as it slips down the wrong pipe. I cough and splutter as Katie looks at me with a cocked brow.

"Aiden and I are friends." I emphasize the word as if she doesn't understand the meaning. "He was just thinking about the poor kids who'd lose all those donations if we told the truth."

Now it's Katie's turn to cough. She thumps her chest with her fist and clears her throat, her face reddening. Something sparkles in the light and catches my eye.

"The kids. Sure, okay. Whatever you want to tell yourself," she says with a wry smile. I don't pay attention, instead I grab her hand and pull her fingers up to my eyeballs for a closer look.

"What is this?" I demand, my face less than an inch away from the diamond on her wedding ring finger. Katie's blush deepens and a little giggle escapes her lips.

"Colin proposed!"

Something squirms in my stomach, and I'm not sure what it is or what it means. We set our drinks on the coffee table and I pull my friend into a bear hug.

"Here I am waffling on about nonsense and you've been hiding this. Katie! This is amazing news."

Katie's beaming now and we break apart, then she holds her hand out for me to inspect the ring. It's a pretty little thing. Modest, prob-ably silver - but the most sparkly diamond I've ever seen.

"Colin deploys in the morning."

Katie's fiancé is in the military. Half the time I forget she's even in a relationship; he's gone so often. My shoulders sag as I look at the shadow of sadness wiping the smile off her face.

"How long is he gone, this time?"

"Six months. He's staying with his parents; they're caring for his grandma and don't expect she'll be around much longer." The words catch in her throat and she blinks away from my gaze. I rub her shoulder and bite my lip. Suddenly my drama, put in perspective, feels small and insignificant.

We spend the rest of the evening watching movies, with me doing my very best to crack jokes in a weak attempt at taking Katie's mind off things.

As the early hours approach, she falls asleep on the couch and I just stare at her in the dark living room. Her face is illuminated by the blue light from the TV. Her words echo in my mind on repeat.

He really has it bad for you.

What makes her think that about Aiden? Can she be right? My imagination runs wild, totally oblivious to the fact that I'm not asleep yet. And yet, maybe I am? Because now I am fantasizing about Aiden dressed up in military gear, pulling me into his arms at the airport and landing a passionate kiss on my lips as everyone stands by, watching.

I relax, my body sinking into the couch. My eyes flutter and a smile creeps over my lips. Katie is so lucky.

I wonder what it would be like to be engaged.

Then I remember: I am.

Right. I need a plan. But my brain is fuzzy, and delirium is beginning to set in. When it's stupid-o-clock, the idea of marrying Aiden doesn't seem so crazy.

I mean, it's for the children, right?

CHAPTER 8

I SIT BOLT UPRIGHT AT THE SOUND OF A
knock on the door. Sunlight pours in through
the windows and Katie is nowhere to be seen.
I rub my eyes with a grumble as the banging
thumps against my temples.

"Who is it?" I moan through a yawn.

The door swings open with a squeal and
reveals Aiden, wearing a dark suit. His eyes
are dark and brooding as he scans the room
then a grim smile crosses his face when he
finds me on the couch.

"You're looking very dapper. What's the
occasion?" I ask, then I realize I probably have
panda eyes. I pat my hair in a feeble attempt

to tame it, but it sits like a brown wiry bird's nest atop my head in a messy bun.

"You won't believe this, but I got a call from the Children's Hospital."

I get up and wring my hands with a laugh. "Oh."

Aiden does not look amused. Instead, he marches over to the kitchen area and changes the coffee filter.

"I need you to get ready. They're expecting us in an hour - and you know how long it's going to take us to get across the city."

My mouth hangs open and I stand rooted on the spot as his words slowly begin to register.

"Why are they expecting us?"

Aiden rubs his forehead with a heavy sigh. "They've been inundated with donations in our names and want us to take a tour of the hospital."

Oh boy.

"How is this happening? - Wait, don't answer that." I wave a hand at him and pace the room, feeling dazed. The longer I leave this, the more tangled the web becomes. "So, what? We have to pretend to be a couple at the hospital now?"

Aiden nods gravely. "I couldn't exactly turn them down, could I?"

We stare at each other for a few moments, blinking in silence while the coffee machine makes a weird sound. A burning smell fills the air and Aiden scrunches up his nose.

"You need a new coffee machine," he says. I shrug at him. "I'll add it to the gift registry."

In normal circumstances, we'd both laugh at that joke. But this is not normal. In fact, my brain is struggling to come up with a memory of a scenario crazier than this one. The only one that comes close is when Aiden and I went to a Halloween party at my office, dressed as Red Riding Hood and the Wolf... and no one else was in costume.

Now that I think about it, I should have known that workplace was never going to be my home. There were so many red flags.

"Look, if you want to call the hospital and explain..."

Aiden's voice breaks into my thoughts and I start shaking my head so fast I worry I'll end up with whiplash. I turn on my heel and dash for the bathroom, shouting over my shoulder.

"Give me ten minutes."

It actually takes me fourteen minutes to

get ready, and by the time I return to my living room, Aiden's forehead is bright red and shiny.

Thankfully, traffic isn't so bad. We manage to catch the subway just as it's departing from the station and we face no delays, which is remarkable in New York. Travelling around the city at any time of day is like moving in slow motion. And yet, this is the second time Aiden and I have broken a travel time record. Or maybe it does take as long as usual and it's just that time flies when I'm around Aiden? It's possible.

"I've gotta be honest… I didn't even know New York had a Children's Hospital. I made that up," I confess as we walk up to the front doors. Aiden makes an exasperated sigh, then he wraps his arm around my waist and settles his hand on my hip. I lurch to the side with a shriek as if I've just been electrocuted.

"What are you doing?" I hiss at him. His warm touch was so unexpected and without warning, my heart is racing. I've even broken into a nervous sweat.

"We're in love, remember? We need to act like a couple just about to get married," Aiden says through gritted teeth, his face fixed into the reddest smile I've ever seen.

I open my mouth and stare at him dumbly, the realization settling.

Oh, that's right… engaged couples like to touch each other in public. PDA is not something of which I am a fan. My last boyfriend, Chuck - oh boy, does that name take me back to the dark ages - he loved to show affection. He even used to rest his head on my shoulder when we sat in the park, or the cinema… or in a taxi. I inwardly shudder at the memory of his greasy hair touching my neck. He needed to go.

Aiden's eyes come back into focus and guilt nips at my insides as I give him an apologetic smile. He's been such a good sport, and all I've been is jumpy and awkward. I'm hardly making his life any easier.

"Right. Sorry, how about we hold hands?" I offer my hand like a peace offering and Aiden gratefully takes it. The touch zings up to my head and makes my mind spin.

With a reassuring nod to each other, we march through the doors, squeezing each other's hand so tight, I'm not sure who's more nervous.

To my utmost shock and horror, a flood of photographers rush in our direction. We barely have a moment to find our bearings before we're blinded by flashes of light.

Someone grasps my free hand and shakes it enthusiastically.

"It's great to meet you. Everyone here at the hospital is so grateful for your generosity."

A mature woman, wearing a white lab coat over a dress, talks a hundred miles an hour as we are guided down the corridor.

"What are all of the cameras for?" Aiden asks in his fake polite voice. It's the one he uses when he wants to make a complaint but doesn't have the heart to do it.

"We called a few tabloids. I never expected the story to be picked up by so many people. But it's not every day a bride and groom ask their guests to donate money to our hospital. You two will be famous by the end of the day."

We stop outside a pair of doors as the woman takes her lanyard and raises it to the lock pad. Aiden and I seize the moment to exchange horrified looks. Aiden doesn't speak, but I can hear his thoughts as loudly as my own.

What are we going to do now?

CHAPTER 9

AFTER VISITING THE HOSPITAL, AIDEN AND I
sit in a busy coffee shop. We're white-faced
and staring at each other, cradling our drinks.
The bustle of people in the crowded shop
blurs in my peripheral vision and my mind
spins.

The hospital had peeling paint in the ceiling. Some of the rooms had broken window
frames. The toys in the playrooms were musty
and stained - probably from decades of drib-
ble. And the beds did not look comfortable.

Yet, every nurse, doctor and child looked
at us with wide, grateful eyes and thanked us
more times than I can count. Seeing how

much the donations mean to them stirred up a mix of emotions.

On the one hand, I'm proud that my outrageous lie has led to something incredibly good. So what if there's no real engagement? The oncology ward is going to get new beds and windows.

"I'm going to ask my Nan if she would get her knitting group to make blankets," I muse aloud. The chief of surgery said they could use some new scanning equipment, and I wonder to myself how much more money we can raise to really make a difference.

But the look of incredulity from Aiden throws me out of my thoughts.

"Are you serious?" he asks, his face growing red. The whites of his knuckles begin to show as he clutches his mug even tighter. "That's what you're thinking, right now?"

I stare at him blankly for a moment. "What?"

Aiden lets go of his mug so fast it's as if he'd been holding a hot plate and only just noticed.

"Emma. Don't you realize what this is?" he whispers, his eyes darting left and right. I follow his line of sight, taking in the fact that we're sitting in a coffee shop together. We've never done that before. Not alone, anyway.

"A… date?"

I regret the words as soon as they leave my mouth because Aiden's face is almost purple now and I worry he's going to explode.

"It's fraud, Emma," Aiden whispers, leaning forward and giving me a piercing look. The judgment in his eyes crush my soul.

Fraud? That's a strong word.

"It's not fraud," I hiss back. "It's a misunderstanding… and anyway, look what good those donations are doing for the hospital."

"We have to tell the truth."

"But the donations? We can't force the hospital to pay them back."

Aiden drags his hand over his face and sighs heavily.

"Let me deal with that. I'll find the money. But please. Just call your parents, talk to Shelly. These lies have to stop."

"You're right," I say in a hollow voice. How could I let myself get so carried away? The fact that the donations were gratefully received by the hospital does not turn my wrong into a right. I need to clear up this mess. "But I can't let you pay for my mistakes. I'll pay you back... as soon as I get another job."

Aiden averts his eyes and picks up his drink again. I gulp mine down, ignoring the terrible burn it leaves as it slides down my throat. Then I start to think of a plan.

"You know who is engaged though," I blurt. Aiden looks at me puzzled. "Katie."

Aiden does not look surprised. "Oh, I know."

I lean forward and study his face. "You knew? He only popped the question last night; how did you find out?"

A guilty grin crosses his face and just the sight of it settles my nerves.

"I helped Colin pick out a ring and booked a reservation at Tortè de Olivia," he said, before taking a sip of his drink. I whistle and sit back in my chair.

"It's impossible to get a reservation there."

Aiden shrugs with an appreciative smile. He's like a little boy who just got an A in his math exam.

"The manager owes me a favor."

I roll my eyes. "That's right, I forgot. It's all about who you know in this city." I finish my drink. "And anyway, I had no idea you were so romantic."

Aiden smirks and a dimple creases in his left cheek.

"There's a lot of things you don't know about me." It's a cheesy line, but it gives me butterflies anyway. We share a moment just gazing into each other's eyes, and I swear his twinkle at me. I am dazzled and totally oblivious to all of life's problems. But then Aiden's face drops and he clears his throat, throwing me out of my daze.

"I've got to go. I'm meeting a potential client later and want to go through my presentation."

I snap my fingers and nod. "Go ahead. Hope it goes better than mine. Who's the client this time?"

Aiden bites his lip as he rises to a stand. "Can't say, but let me tell you this: if I land this one, I can retire early."

We gather our belongings and walk to the door, bumping shoulders with the people in the crowded coffee shop.

"So, what are you going to do?" Aiden asks me as I press my lips against his cheek.

"Colin was deployed today, so Katie will need some comfort food," I begin. Then I catch the look of concern that has washed over Aiden's chiselled face. "But first, I need to drop in and see my parents," I say brightly, catching onto his thoughts.

Relief washes away his concern and Aiden sighs, pressing a hand over his heart.

"I'm proud of you. Let me know how it goes, okay?"

I nod as we start walking in opposite directions.

"Good luck with your presentation. I'm sure you'll knock it out of the park." I pump my fist in the air. His face flushes with color and my heart squeezes. Flashbacks flood my mind of him reading to the kids at the hospital, asking them questions and cracking jokes. He's quite possibly the most genuinely nice person in the city. Maybe the whole planet.

My stomach lurches as I flag down a cab. Meanwhile, I have to go confess my sins to my doting parents and tell them I'm not marrying him after all.

Ironically, days like these would call for a

dress fitting to lift the mood. But right now I'm pretty sure I shouldn't be seen within ten feet of a bridal store.

I make a mental note to pick up donuts on the way home.

And ice-cream. Lots and lots of ice-cream.

CHAPTER 10

My mom always taught me it's rude to turn up unannounced and empty-handed. So, I call ahead. She sounds far too happy for my liking. Her excitement is almost tangible, like a pair of hands that stretch out of the speaker and tighten themselves around my jugular.

I pick up the biggest bunch of sunflowers I can find and a box of Belgium chocolates.

But as I stand on the doorstep to my parents' house, I start to rethink my choice of gifts. I look like I'm going on a date.

Whenever mom has bad news to share, she brings me presents. When my goldfish, Wally, died, she gave me a pair of plastic heel shoes. They had a giant red bow on the front and the heels were bedazzled with fake diamonds. They were the most uncomfortable, impractical shoes on the planet, but I loved those shoes. When my bunny, Flopsy, died, I got a bunch of stick-on earrings. They were amazing. Growing up in the 90s was awesome. Thinking back on my childhood, though, reminds me of why I do not have pets.

Mom answers the door, shrugging a phone to her ear as she waves me in.

"Yes, I'll hold." She leans to me as she closes the door and whispers, "Your dad is asleep. He just got back from a nightshift not too long ago."

I nod, my knotted stomach loosening with blessed relief. It's only my mom who I have to face up to. She can pass on the message, and I'll be spared the look of utter devastation on my dad's face. At least, for now.

I walk into the kitchen and pull out a crystal vase, trying not to eavesdrop as my mom jabbers into her phone at top speed. She mentions the word flowers and my stomach churns again. Please don't be about my wedding.

"April eleventh. That's right... I know it's short notice."

What are the odds that there is another big event requiring flowers on the same day as my fictional wedding? I busy myself with the sunflowers and try to think about how I'm going to break the news.

But the words only come in fragments, like pieces of a jigsaw puzzle, and none of them fit together. Shelly… dress… fiancé… news.

I take a low deep breath, and swallow hard. Don't over-think it, Emma, just come out with it. Like dad says… when you have to do something you hate, do it fast. It's like ripping off a band-aid.

"Sorry about that. Are those for me?"

My mom is back and my ears ring so loudly I can hardly hear her voice. I take another breath as my arms tingle; a rising numbness reaches my shoulders and for a second I think I'm actually going to pass out. Aiden is allergic to telling lies, am I allergic to telling the truth?

"Mumihavetosaysomethingaboutthewedding," I say in a single breath. Only, the words come out like gobbledegook and my mom just stares at me with a frown.

"What?"

I grab a glass and gesture to it with my other hand. "Do you mind?"

My mom continues to watch me, her eyes like lasers burning into my soul as I fill the glass to the brim and gulp the water before taking another breath. It's so hot. I shrug off my jacket and drag a hand through my hair.

"Are you feeling okay? You look clammy." My mom reaches out for my head but I back away.

"I'm fine, it's just a hot day," I insist. Fanning myself with a hand.

My mom makes that humming sound she makes when she doesn't believe something. How is it so hard to believe I'm just hot - on a crisp January day - but easy to buy the lie that I have been secretly planning a wedding?

Don't answer that.

"Mom, listen. I need to talk to you about Aiden," I say in my best impression of a serious, mature woman. But the way my mom looks at me, with glassy eyes and cheeks dimpling, I swear she still sees me as that little girl in plastic shoes with sticker earrings.

"I—" Before I can say another syllable, the doorbell rings and I can't decide if I'm relieved or irritated. This is agony, and now we're just delaying the inevitable.

"Just a second, let me get that." My mom disappears from the kitchen while I refill my glass.

"Lizzie! What a surprise, come on in. Emma's in the kitchen."

I freeze with the cold glass pressed against my lips as my heart races. Lizzie? No, this can't be Lizzie Carmichael, the biggest gossip in my mom's social circle? She's chairman of the you-name-it committee. With her perfect golf-playing husband, and her perfect children, all of them playing house in their mansion surrounded by white picket fencing.

Every visit leaves a bitter taste; she drops passive-aggressive comments like stink bombs. All the while raving about how blessed she is and how strange it is that she doesn't have any problems. Then she ends the agonizing experience with a single look. Eyes drooping, lips pouting and a slight incline of the head. Pity.

That, is Lizzie Carmichael.

And not only that, but she's Shelly's aunt.

My mom enters with a pale face and wide eyes. She looks at me with so much intent, I think she's trying to send me a telepathic message. As if there is a secret radio wave that just the two of us tap into. But alas, there isn't one, and I just stare at her blankly, as nothing comes to mind. Instead, a dark-haired woman enters, not a spot of gray on her. Even I have a few grays. She's about the same age as my mom, but her face is plump and youthful. There's an annoying dewiness about her countenance and she looks at me with a glittering smile, flashing brilliantly white veneers.

"Emma, sweetheart! I thought I saw you. Still driving a Yaris, I see? Mela, darling. When are you and Ted going to buy your daughter a real car? I just put a deposit on the new Tesla for Jimmy. Good for the environment and has its own karaoke machine too."

My mom and I wear a matching grin. The kind that fixes unnaturally wide and never reaches the eyes.

But our inauthenticity is supposedly missed, as Lizzie pulls me in for a hug, undeterred. I resist the urge to choke on her musky scent, but the jolt in my shoulders must give me away because Lizzie pulls back and surveys me with mild alarm.

"I'm sorry, is my perfume too strong? I was shopping in the Short Hills mall with

Jennifer Aniston this morning and she wanted to test the new Gucci fragrance. I told her it was too potent."

My mom and I glance at each other. Another thing about Lizzie - she embellishes. Last week, she was making bread with Paula Deen. Before that, she was doing hot yoga with Kris Jenner. Six months ago, she went on a girls' trip to the Dominican with Meryl Streep, Helen Mirren and Judy Dench, where they all discussed global warming and talked about shooting a movie to raise awareness and donate all of the proceeds to charity.

She would have no problem telling all her friends about a fancy fake wedding at the plaza hotel. Although, if she was me, she would have definitely insisted that Elton John was going to sing at the reception, and *Nicholas Sparks' has been so inspired by our romance, he's writing his next book all about us.*

It's going to make him billions.

Go big, or go home right?

I glance at the small clock ticking in the corner and notice that almost ten minutes have passed while I've been stuck in my head. Lizzie and my mom lean against the breakfast bar talking. I smile and nod like a puppet.

"Let me give you my maid's number, you should fire yours. This won't do at all." Lizzie runs her index finger along the granite worktop and brushes her fingers with her nose pinched. My nostrils flare as I catch the rush of pink flooding my mom's cheeks. My parents don't have a maid, and Lizzie knows it.

"What brings you to our humble home?" my mom asks. I drum my fingers on the counter and chew my lip as I wonder why my mom has anything to do with this woman. But my mom is the gentlest soul in the world. She's the type of person who would pick up and cuddle a skunk while the rest of the world runs off screaming. She sees the good in people. All people.

Remembering that gives me hope that once the truth is out, she might still love me.

"You may have heard my favorite niece is getting married. Their announcement is on page six of the New York Times, you know." Lizzie pulls out an envelope from her bag and thrusts it in my mom's bewildered face.

"In case you were wondering… yes. That's gold leaf paper imported from Venice. And if you smell it, that's the scent of an ancient spice from a small tribe in Yemen. Locals believe it to give good fortune."

Half of me wants to laugh. But the other half wants to snatch the paper and give it a good sniff. I need all the luck I can get.

"Well, I appreciate the invite Lizzie. And we love Shelly, of course. But we cannot attend the wedding." My mom looks pointedly at me. This is the part where I'm supposed to bashfully wring my hands and say, "You know what? I'm not getting married, I just made that up."

But then I have visions of Lizzie throwing her hands in the air with an exclamation. Her dark eyes twinkling as her devious mind draws up a list of contacts to share this salacious gossip with.

My gaze flickers to my mom and something stirs inside of me. Lizzie will never let us live this down, my mom will be subject to her taunts for the rest of her life. And we'd have to go to Shelly's wedding. I turn to Lizzie and my face breaks into a wicked grin as I prepare to, once again, lie like I've never lied before.

"They say great minds think alike. Shelly and I have picked the same day to get married."

They also say fools seldom differ, but I don't mention that.

"I wish I could change it, but Perrier Francè has a very strict schedule."

"Perrier Francè? Good grief. How did you…"

"He's a friend of a friend." I wave my hand and catch my mother's look of surprise with a twinge of guilt. "Vera Wang has designed my dress. I said to Aiden - he's my fiancé - darling, this is all too much. But he just keeps saying, 'You deserve nothing but the best, my love.' And there is simply no point in arguing with him."

Lizzie's eyes look at my left hand, and I suddenly become aware of the naked finger that should be sporting a massive rock. Lizzie looks dazed but shakes her head a little, as if brushing away her thoughts.

"How… charming. I am hosting Shelly and Frederick's engagement party at my house this weekend. Please come, bring your fiancé too, I must meet this lovely man."

My mom jumps in with a delighted squeal. "We'd love to be there."

I grit my teeth. Aiden will kill me when I tell him about this.

"Of course," I say tensely. "Anyway, I best go. I'll let you two ladies talk about weddings. Lots to do!"

I shoot my mom a quick look of apology before I pull her in for a hug, and she just stares at me stunned. Then I turn to Lizzie.

"Lovely seeing you again, Lizzie." We exchange cheek kisses as if we're in an extravagant villa in France. Then I walk out and do not look back.

But just before I open the front door, I cannot mistake Lizzie's strangled voice.

"Honestly, I didn't think your Emma would survive in the city. But look at her now! Marrying a rich businessman and working for the top shoe designer in the city. You must be happy."

I freeze with my hand on the door handle and wait for my mom to set her straight, telling her I got fired from the amazing job. But to my surprise, she doesn't.

"Oh, I am so proud." She says simply instead.

CHAPTER 11

I COME BACK TO MY APARTMENT TO FIND IT sparkling clean, which tells me one thing: Katie is home, and she's upset. Josh Groban is on the stereo, singing the saddest, most depressing song on the planet. The cookie candle I bought her for Christmas sits alight on the countertop.

"Katie, I've got ice-cream."

When there's no response, I creep to her bedroom door and push it open a crack. "Hey, are you in here?"

The door swings fully open and I struggle to hold back a gasp. Every single box, cupboard and drawer has been emptied all over the floor. I can't even see the color of the carpet. Or is it tile? I forget.

Katie's flushed face pops up from behind the bed and she beams at me. "Hi, I didn't hear you come in," she says in a breezy voice.

"I thought we already did the Marie Kondo thing to start off the year." I stay in the doorway and scan the piles and piles of junk. Katie and I have this ever-running goal to be minimalists. But clearly, we still have some work to do.

"I was just freshening everything up. You know, giving things a home and cleaning the baseboards." Katie stands and picks up a file from her bed. "I made a list of jobs for you, by the way. The contact names and phone numbers are at the back."

I take the file and flip through the pages. There must be more than a hundred listings.

"Katie, you didn't have to- "

"Yes, I did," she interjects. Her eyes are glassy, and I get the impression she's holding back tears.

"Is this about Colin?" I ask carefully. Katie shakes her head so violently her hair falls out of its bun and hangs in a messy spray across her shoulders. I tilt my head as I study my friend. No matter how hard she tries to put on a brave face, the hurt is written all over it.

"Come here," I spread my arms, and she stumbles through the piles of stuff into my hug. "What's going on?"

Katie sniffs into my shoulder while I stroke her hair.

"Colin's grandma had a fall, and his mom is out of town. She's asked me to stay with her for a while once she's out of hospital."

I pat her back with a hum as I process the news. Once again, Katie's problems put my own into perspective.

"I want to be there for Colin's grandma, because he's away. But I don't know if I can do this. I've never been responsible for anyone, before. What if I make her tea wrong? Or poison her food?"

I pull back to look in her teary eyes. "That's impossible. You're not capable of doing anything awful, you're the sweetest person ever." Tear drops leak out of Katie's eyes and lines of mascara roll down her cheeks.

"I'm already packed, so I just need to keep busy while I wait for the call." She gestures to the messy room and I nod.

"Any ideas when that might be?" I ask. She shakes her head with a sigh.

"Could be any time."

I chew my lip as I take it in. But before I can say anything, the front door opens with a bang and I hear Aiden shouting.

"We're in Katie's room," I shout back. Hurried footsteps approach, and then Aiden's flustered face comes into view as he beams at me.

"I got it. Emma, I got the client," he says with his cheeks flushed. He lifts me up in his burly arms and throws me around in a circle as I squeal back. The way his strong hands cinch in my waist gives me tingles. I rest my hands around his neck and squeeze, my whole body warming. But the celebration is short-lived as he sets me down and looks at Katie.

"Are you okay?"

Katie nods far too enthusiastically to come across as authentic. Besides, the black lines on her cheeks say it all. Aiden pulls out a hand-kerchief from the pocket of his suit jacket and offers it to her. The simple act makes me all gooey inside. What man carries a handker-chief these days? With the shine of his black hair and his dimpled chin, I have visions of

Cary Grant offering Deborah Kerr his hand-kerchief in An Affair to Remember.

And for a split second, a twinge of unease nips at my stomach.

"Katie has had a stressful day," I say. "But look what she's put together." I hold out the file for Aiden, he looks at it and his brows raise.

"A list of designer firms?"

Katie dabs her face and nods with a hiccup. "For Emma."

Aiden rests a hand over his heart, as if warmed by the gesture. Then he gives her shoulder a squeeze.

"I'm sorry you've had a tough day. I hear congratulations are in order, though?" His words prompt a small smile from Katie as she shows him her ring. He nods with approval. "Colin is a very lucky man."

Katie beams. "I guess we're all engaged, now!"

Aiden shakes his head with a laugh and glances at me. I stare back. Oh man. Here it comes. The moment I have to tell him we're still engaged, and now we've been invited to Shelly's engagement party. But my confession is delayed by the sweet sound of Aiden's phone ringing.

"I need to take this." He raises a finger and marches out of the hall, leaving me to reel in my thoughts.

"Katie, Aiden and I were at the Children's Hospital today," I say, Katie smirks and pulls out her phone from her jeans.

"I know," she says simply. Then she taps on her screen and holds it up for me to see a picture of Aiden and I grinning sheepishly with our arms wrapped around each other. "You're all over the news."

I swallow against a lump in my throat as I read the story.

"They make us sound like saints," I say through a breath.

Katie rubs my arm and looks at me with sympathy.

"To that hospital, you are. Look how many children you've already helped. They're going to renovate a ward, and with their new scanner, they'll be able to diagnose cancer so much faster. Early treatment is paramount to fighting the disease."

I frown at her. "It doesn't justify lying,

though. I mean… isn't it fraud to accept donations in this situation?"

Katie doesn't answer and I see the conflict in her eyes. I wonder how many good deeds I'll need to do to finally get rid of the sickly feeling in my stomach. Maybe I should join the Peace Corps?

"Hey Emma. Can I talk to you for a minute?" I bite my lip at the sound of Aiden's strangled shout.

"He's probably seen the news," I whisper to Katie. She raises her hands and backs into her room again, tripping over a rolled-up blanket. "Good luck. I'll be in here if you need me."

I turn on the spot and take a deep breath to steal some courage.

I enter the living room. Aiden is standing by the window with a dark expression on his face. He fixes a pair of brooding eyes on me and stuffs a hand in his pocket. Suddenly, I feel small. Like I'm a child at the headmaster's office, about to get detention.

"That was my new client."

I lower to sit on the couch, pinching my brows, wondering where Aiden is going with this.

"Did he back out of the contract?" I ask. Aiden walks over to me and sits on the coffee table. With a shake of his head, he reaches for my hands and looks deeply into my eyes.

"I know you've just told your parents about...the lie," he glances away and shuts his eyes for a moment. Then he squeezes my hands and looks at me again, with renewed strength. "But I need a favor."

"Anything," I say and bolt into an upright sitting position. My stomach tightens. After everything he's done for me recently, I owe Aiden a million favors. "What do you need?"

Aiden tilts his head and looks up through his dark lashes. His lips pout. It's the perfect smolder, and it gives me chills.

"I need you to come with me to Hawaii this weekend to meet him and his wife."

I turn my head as I study him with narrowed eyes. "Okay..."

Aiden squeezes my hands again. "As my fiancé."

CHAPTER 12

"WAIT. I'M CONFUSED. ARE YOU MARRYING Aiden?"

"No."

Katie frowns and stares at me. Her mouth is full of chocolate ice-cream. "But you're still pretending to be engaged?"

I nod and dig my spoon into the tub of vanilla ice-cream in front of me. My mind is still spinning. Aiden and I talked for an hour, then he got another work call and had to leave. Considering the 'favor' he needed, he was relieved that I hadn't let the cat out of the bag to my parents just yet.

"We made a deal. He's going to come with me to Shelly's engagement party. Then we're going to Hawaii to meet with his client."

Katie swallows and pinches her nose as if struck by brain freeze. "So, you're still pretending to be engaged? What about April eleventh? Are you going to change the date?"

I sigh heavily. "If I do that, I'll have to go to insufferable Shelly's wedding."

Katie looks at me like I'm crazy. But she's not tearful anymore, and the last time her phone pinged she didn't jump and turn pale. Which means that my ridiculously poor decision making has taken her mind off things.

"What will you do after that?"

I shrug. At this point, Aiden and I are just taking things one day at a time.

"Why does Aiden's client want to meet you?" Katie asks, setting her bowl down.

"He saw us on the news. According to Aiden, it was one of the reasons why he got the contract. So, we need to be pretty convincing."

"Convincing?" Katie smirks. "That'll be easy."

"What do you mean?" I ask as she picks up the remote and slides through the movie listings on TV. Katie laughs.

"You and Aiden have been flirting shame-lessly since day one. Don't pretend to deny it."

My face burns as I make exclamations back. "That's not true!" Sure, I have a crush on him. But it takes two to tango, and he doesn't see me that way. "We're just friends."

"Men and women can't be friends."

I cross my arms. "Oh yeah? Are you and Aiden mortal enemies? Or are you cheating on Colin?"

Katie's shoulders shake as she chuckles at my question.

"That's different. Aiden and I talk about superficial things, like the weather. You two confide in each other."

I can't argue with that. More than a few times, we've stayed up late talking about everything and anything. Philosophy, religion, politics. True love. There are no forbidden topics between us. Whenever I get into a bind, Aiden's the first person I call.

"He's never asked me out or kissed me. It's been five years... how do you make a move after so long?"

And what if we did try to be in a relation-ship and it ends badly? I'll lose a best friend. Forever.

"And yet, he's happily gone along with this fake wedding charade and he's taking you to Hawaii on a romantic getaway," Katie shoots back. Then she settles on a movie, My Best Friend's Wedding. I roll my eyes.

"Not this one. It doesn't have a happy ending," I protest. Katie sits up and her mouth hangs open. I sense a rant brewing. But instead of unleashing one, she makes a statement.

"I should have known you'd be rooting for Julia Roberts."

"Who wouldn't?" I say with a shrug. "Besides... she's his best friend. Cameron Diaz is just this rich daddy's girl with no personality. Julia is flawed and intelligent and..."

I stop at the unimpressed look on my friend's face.

"You think you're Julia Roberts, don't you?"

I stare back in stunned silence as the opening song plays.

"No," I say finally. Katie points at me, her polished nail shining in the glow of the TV.

"You should learn from this movie," she said seriously. "See what happens when you don't share your feelings with the one you love? If you don't say anything, someday Aiden will go and find a young woman from Idaho and get married six weeks later."

I fake a laugh. Preposterous! Aiden wouldn't do that. Anyway, he hates potatoes.

"Laugh all you want, but I'm telling you. What if the only person you're lying to, is yourself?"

Her words hit my ears like a hurricane, the force nearly throwing me back. A phone rings and the two of us gulp and exchange looks. She picks it up like it's about to explode and I hold my breath.

"Is it…?"

She nods, ashen-faced and jumps to her feet as she answers the call.

"Hey, is it time?"

I hastily grab the remote and mute the TV as Katie talks on the phone. Then she ends the call and looks at me with terror. "They want me to go to her condo right now."

A bolt of nerves rush through my entire body, as if I'm the one going to care for Colin's grandma for an unknown period of time. I try to jump to my feet, but I wobble on my legs like a jellyfish out of water.

"I'll drive you," I blurt, and I grab my jacket. But Katie backs away, shaking her head.

"No, you stay here and relax. I need to be grown up about this. I mean, she's Colin's grandma, and it'll only be a few days, right? How hard can it be?"

I try to argue back but Katie insists on it. She rushes about, collects her things and leaves without another word.

Being alone in the apartment again leaves me with a heavy heart. No longer in the mood to watch a romantic comedy, I switch off the TV and run a hot bath instead. Katie has this unique ability to cut through any drama and get to the root of a situation. She's never been afraid of the heavy stuff. Maybe there is a part of me that is enjoying this game of I'm-getting-married-to-my-crush.

But it's a dangerous game, one that is doomed to end with a broken heart. My mom often says 'the truth will always come out.' So it's only a matter of time before this house of cards comes crashing down.

But then, Aiden needs me. Sure it means I have to keep lying to everyone, but I made a promise.

And I never go back on a promise.

CHAPTER 13

I'M A BALL OF JITTERS DURING THE ENTIRE CAR ride and I keep glancing at my phone. No messages. Aiden parks and takes my hand, giving it a squeeze.

"Heard anything from Katie, yet?" he asks. I close my eyes with a shaky breath, unable to answer.

"I think I'm having a panic attack," I whisper. Cold numbness is spreading from my arms to my chest. With my eyes closed, I tune in to the chatter from the people milling around the car. A clink of metal and the brush of cotton against the squeaky leather tells me Aiden has unbuckled his seatbelt. Before I know it, I'm flung into his shoulder. He encircles my panicked body with his arms and holds me so tight, it's as if he's trying to hold me together. I nuzzle his neck and inhale the woody scent of his cologne. It's grounding. And just like that, the numbness evaporates. My arms tingle as the feeling returns to my fingers and for a second, I forget where we are and what we're doing.

"It's going to be okay," Aiden says with warmth. His deep voice rumbles against my head and I can't stop the small smile creeping across my lips. I pull back to look into his sincere eyes and nip my bottom lip.

"I hate being in the dark. It's been two days… and I've heard nothing from her."

Aiden's brows knit together. Then he reaches inside his jacket pocket.

"I'm sure she's just busy. Right now, we need to focus on what we need to do." He pulls out a small blue box wrapped with white ribbon tied in a pretty bow.

"This is for you."

My breath hitches as I take the box in my hands. It's heavier than it looks. "What is it?"

I look up to catch the smirk on Aiden's face.

"What do you think it is? Open it."

I fumble with the ribbon and flip the box open. A flash of light blinds me and a thought crosses my mind that this is a practical joke. As I jerk my wrist, the light moves away from my eyes and I study the beautiful engagement ring staring at me.

"It's platinum, I know you hate silver." Aiden says, rubbing his neck. I frown at him. I don't hate silver. That makes me sound like a spoilt brat. I just hate it that my silver necklaces tarnish when I leave them on the sink in the bathroom.

"The diamond is 1.5 carat," Aiden continues with his cheeks reddening. I look down at the ring again, the single diamond is so shiny, every time I angle it towards my face, I'm blinded.

"Well? Do you like it?" Aiden asks. Before I know what I'm doing, I'm bobbing my head with a goofy grin.

"It's gorgeous." I slip it on my finger and hold out my hand to inspect it. "It's a perfect fit... how did you know my size?"

Aiden's whole face is crimson now. "I called your mom."

This feels all-too real and a giddiness rushes over me as I take in the moment. But I can't get carried away. This is just an act; we're not really getting married.

"I'll be really careful with it. So you can return it when this is all done," I say with earnest. A flash behind Aiden's eyes gives me pause, and I can't help but notice the corners of his mouth drop. But before I can question him on it, a woman knocks on the window and Aiden recovers his smile.

"Your car is fogging up. You're not getting up to no good in there, are you?" It's Shelly. Even with the fogged-up glass obscuring her face, her mass of blonde hair gives her away. Besides, it's impossible to mistake that high pitched voice. Aiden takes my hand as I brush off my cocktail dress and we both inhale deeply.

"Showtime," Aiden whispers.

"This was a bad idea," Aiden mumbles through a fake smile as we stand rigid, like a pair of celebrities in a crowd of paparazzi. All of Shelly's friends and family swan around us, throwing compliments, taking the spotlight away from Shelly and Frederick. Even her aunt Lizzie shoulders her way in to introduce herself to Aiden.

"Echanté," she says, holding out her hand like she expects him to bow and kiss her rings. "Aiden, I have heard so much about you."

There's an awkward silence as Aiden takes her hand and glances at me. Then I come to my senses.

"Oh, right. Lizzie Carmichael, this is Aiden Daniels."

I'm no good at formalities. I wave my hand limply with a bob of the head in a vain attempt to sound like I know what I'm doing. But there are so many nuances when it comes to social settings, and no one gave me a rule book, so I'm pretty sure I'm breaking at least three of them every minute without even knowing it. Aiden and Lizzie have a polite conversation while I zone out and count the minutes until we are able to leave. She brushes his arm and giggles. The sound makes my skin crawl.

Shelly appears through the crowd, her action-figure fiancé in tow.

"Emma, meet Frederick."

"Hi there, Emma. I've heard a lot about you."

He captures my hand with both of his and shakes it with so much enthusiasm and strength, it almost knocks me off my feet. I have visions of myself flying through the roof like a cartoon character.

"Not too many bad things, I hope," I say with a hearty laugh.

"No, of course not." Though his smile doesn't quite reach his eyes. "Shelly tells me you were in the Peace Corps."

I take a sip of my drink. Did I say that to her? I know I thought about it. Wow. I've told so many lies, I'm losing track. Now I know why my dad always says that good liars have remarkable memory recall.

"I hear you build schoolhouses in Africa. Tell me about that," I say, brightly. I did read a book once on how to be a good conversationalist. Ironically, it's not by talking. Instead, you have to ask lots of questions and do all the listening. I hope by steering the conversation back to Frederick, he'll ask less questions about me. And it works. Shelly's face brightens, and she rests a hand on his chest as she takes over.

"Building is only half of it. Tell them

about the time you saved the little girl from the pack of hyenas."

The crowd of guests turn their attention to Frederick, who launches into his story. With Shelly's help, he soon launches into another one. And another. Each tale taller than the last.

A break in the crowd reveals my mom speaking to Lizzie. I turn to Aiden.

"Wanna sneak out of here? I think we've shown our faces long enough."

He nods. "I thought you'd never ask."

I agree to meet him at the car before wading my way through the people, just as Frederick re-enacts his wrestling match with a lion. The guests make sounds of awe, as if not aware of how far-fetched the story is - or maybe too intoxicated to care.

"There you are Emma." My mom pulls me in for a quick hug then whispers frantically in my ear. "Don't leave me with her."

Guilt nips at my side as I give her an apologetic smile.

"Aiden and I have a flight to catch," I explain. "I'm sorry I can't go cake tasting this weekend."

My mom does little to hide the disappointment on her face, but curiosity takes over. "Where are you going?"

It's not like me to take impromptu trips. Lizzie stares at me with such intensity, it's as if she's worried she might not catch my reply if she blinks.

"Hawaii. We're spending the weekend with one of Aiden's clients."

"My goodness," Lizzie says in a revered tone, her fingers flying to rest on her collarbone. "What does Aiden do for these clients to warrant such a trip?"

I puff out my cheeks and exhale. Computer stuff? I have no idea. Aiden has tried to tell Katie and me about his work on more than one occasion, but as soon as words like systems, security and data hit my brain, I've gone off to a dream world.

"He works with technology, for corporate clients. You know, to um... protect systems, and analyze their gobo-gammas to make sure there aren't any diseases - no, sorry, I mean viruses."

Lizzie's eyes are nearly as wide as my mother's.

"Gobo-gammas?" Lizzie repeats. Heat rises to my face and I resist dabbing the drops of perspiration clinging to my temples.

"It's very high-level stuff. Not many people even know about it."

I think I've just about fooled Lizzie, but my mom's cheeks pinch and she tries to conceal her laugh with a coughing fit. "Well, be safe and have a fun time."

We hug again but this time she squeezes a little tighter.

"Love you mom." We break apart. "Thanks for inviting us, Lizzie. I hope the wedding goes well."

Lizzie's face breaks into a beam. "That reminds me, my husband, Stuart, he called in a favor and got the last conference room at the plaza hotel."

My heartbeat booms in my ears so loudly, I wonder if anyone else can hear it, and drops of sweat roll down my cheeks.

To make things a million times worse, Shelly is back. By the look on her face, she's caught the tail end of our conversation. She taps her glass with a spoon and the sound rings in a silence from the guests.

"Thank you so much to everyone for coming tonight. Frederick and I cannot wait to share our special day with you all. Now, I know you've all been delighted to meet Emma and Aiden. So, I'm excited to announce this... Emma and Aiden are getting married at the Plaza on the same day as us. So, we'll be seeing you two-" Shelly's gaze hovers over me, every glittering tooth on display. "On April eleventh at the Plaza. Here's to us!"

My mom gawks at me as the room explodes into cheers. She leans in. "You're getting married at the Plaza?"

And here I was thinking things couldn't get any worse. They have.

CHAPTER 14

I'VE NEVER BEEN TO HAWAII BEFORE. AS THE
plane begins its descent, I peer out of the
window to glimpse the island. But it's dark.
Unlike the soft orange glow over New York,
there are only a few twinkling lights, like stars,
dotted below.

"So, what's the plan?" I ask, turning back
to Aiden. He pulls a headphone away from his
ear and drags his gaze from the TV screen to
look at me.

"Plan? Oh... right." He scratches his chin
and laughs with his eyes cast downward, as if
the grand plan might be written on his lap
belt.

"You don't have a plan, do you?" I say,

crossing my arms. "Tell me then, who is this bigshot client?"

"His name is Bill—"

"—Gates?" I finish, shocked. Aiden breaks into a laugh.

"No. Not Bill Gates." He picks up his glass and takes a swig. "Bill Fitzgerald. He's the owner of a security tech firm and wants me to be his technical solution designer."

Aiden stops, catching the blank look on my face. He sighs. "I'll be working in presales, helping new companies find solutions using Mr. Fitzgerald's security software."

He speaks as if this should make any sense to me, so to spare myself an eye-roll and further computer talk, I put on my best poker face and nod.

"Right, got it."

I sincerely hope there will be no computer questions during this trip. I'm pretty sure I won't be able to get away with making up words like gobo-gamma to Mr. Fitzgerald.

"What's the point of this trip, then?"

Aiden takes my hand and gives it a squeeze.

"I'm not sure. But when someone invites

you to an all-expenses paid trip to Hawaii for the weekend, you don't say no."

"Really? What if he is a mafia boss and we end up getting tangled in a plot to smuggle drugs back to New York?"

"The only thing we're getting tangled up in, is all the lies you've been telling."

Ouch. I guess the truth really does hurt.

"Hey, you asked me to come and pretend to be your fiancé," I point out, frowning at him. Aiden raises his hands.

"True. I'm sorry. As soon as this weekend is over, we can come clean and move on."

The plane bumps along the runway so suddenly, I grip Aiden's kneecap for dear life and hold my breath.

"Don't worry," he says in a soothing voice. He wraps his arms around me and kisses the top of my head while rubbing my back. "Everything will be okay. I promise."

The taxi pulls up outside a large hotel; it's all lit up and palm trees line the road. As Aiden helps me out, a flood of music fills my ears and I cannot stop myself from smiling. The upbeat tunes sound tropical. I can't pinpoint the instruments. Bongos maybe. A xylophone?

A curvy Hawaiian woman greets us by the door and places a garland of yellow flowers over my head.

"Welcome to Hawaii," she says in a beautiful accent. Each syllable sounds like a melody coming from her dark lips. I am entranced in a spell. If I had worries, they are now gone. The man at the reception desk gives me the broadest smile and I mirror it, my hips now swaying to the music.

"I love these flower necklaces," I muse, as Aiden rummages in his jacket pocket. The white-haired man at reception chuckles. "It is called a Leis. They're made with yellow hibiscus flowers picked less than a mile from this resort."

I make a noise of awe as I graze one of the smooth petals with my thumb.

"Beautiful." I incline my head with a slight bow. It seems like the right thing to do, but the slight crease forming between the attendant's brows has me doubting myself. Maybe I'm coming across as sarcastic? Great. I've been in Hawaii for two minutes and I've already offended someone.

"Ah. I see you are with Mr. and Mrs. Fitzgerald. You have the honeymoon suite, with an ocean view. Please, if you follow Talisha, she will take you there. If you require any help, please do not hesitate to call the front desk."

The Hawaiian woman joins us as a porter takes our bags and places them on a brass luggage cart.

"I feel like a famous person; I've never known such luxury!" I whisper into Aiden's ear as we follow Talisha.

The dimple creasing in Aiden's cheek is the only response I get as he remains quiet.

Talisha reels off all the general hotel information at lightning speed. But her voice is so heavenly, I barely take in a word. Then we stop outside a white door. With a beep, it swings open and my mouth drops as we step inside.

"Mr. Fitzgerald expects you to join him at breakfast."

I jolt out of my daze just in time to wave as Talisha and the porter disappear behind the door and we are left alone.

"Wow. This is our room? It's huge!" I kick off my sandals and run over to the giant, super-king, four-poster bed and jump onto it. "Check me out, I'm making bed angels," I say fanning my arms and legs. I prop myself up on my elbows and catch Aiden laughing to himself as he loosens his tie.

"I'm glad you're feeling comfortable," he says. I collapse onto my back again and inhale the sweet floral aroma of the hibiscus flowers. I blink up at the dazzling lights in the ceiling.

"Why wouldn't I be comfortable? This is amazing."

As Aiden's face appears in my view, I roll onto my side to grin at him but my stomach flips as I take in his bare torso.

"Why have you always got your shirt off?" I blurt. My heart flutters in my chest as Aiden continues to undress in front of me. He jabs his thumb in the direction of a hot tub sitting in front of the bed.

"I don't know about you, but I think it's customary to remove clothes before you sit in a hot tub."

A rush of heat floods my cheeks and I bury my face into the plush pillows with a giggle. I'm in a five-star resort with Aiden. Sexy boy-next-door Aiden. My fake fiancé. Yes, he's shirtless and we're completely unsupervised. But that doesn't mean I can think about him like this. He's my friend. Just my friend.

A splash has me sitting up again. Aiden moans in such a tantalizing way, it should be made illegal. Then he slides lower into the hot tub until the bubbling water rises to his chin.

Well, at least he's not on show anymore. But just as the thought crosses my mind, he rests his arms on the edge of the tub, and my eyes trace the outline of his muscles, as if drawing a mountainous landscape. Or manscape, rather.

Gosh, he's beautiful. His slick black hair has a few bubbles in it. I want to run my fingers over every chiselled part of his handsome face. He moans again and I don't know if I like what the sound does to me.

No, Emma. Behave yourself!

I'm staring and that's completely inappropriate. But there's something about this place. Hawaii. Ever since we landed, I've felt relaxed, free… mischievous. Besides, Aiden is so kind and caring. He's always been there for me. I feel safe when I'm with him.

I imagine if he opened his eyes, what I must look like to him, curled up on the bed, with my hands clasped under my chin, sighing dreamily as I stare in his direction.

Get a grip!

"Do you want to come in? The water is nice and hot, it's very soothing on the muscles," Aiden says with his eyes still closed. My stomach tightens.

Yes, please.

"NO!"

Aiden's eyes fly open as I clamp my hands over my mouth. "Sorry," I force myself to say. "I'm just super tired. And we've got an early wake up call. So... I better just... Um..."

I look anywhere but at Aiden as the words tumble out of me. I deliver the excuse with as much grace as a baby deer trying to walk for the first time.

"You're right, we should get ready for bed." Aiden rises to a stand and masses of water cascade off his body, like he's a ridiculously gorgeous waterfall. I stand and gawp for a moment. Then, I leap off the bed and bolt for the bathroom.

"Emma, are you okay?"

Aiden knocks on the door as I press my back up to it and hold my breath. It's a crush. Just a silly crush. But hiding it from Aiden in this situation is near impossible. And if I make a move and he doesn't reciprocate, I'll have to suffer the rest of this trip feeling like a first-class idiot.

"I'm sick. Must have been the shrimp at the party."

I make a fake moan and stagger away from the door.

"Do you want me to call for a doctor?"

"No, no. I'll be fine. You go to bed. I'll be in here for a while."

If there's anything to kill the mood, a fake case of food poisoning will do the trick. My plan works. After a quick "Goodnight," I hear Aiden walking away from the door.

Now, I just have to wait until he's asleep before crawling into bed.

A couple of hours pass, and I rearrange the towels and complimentary toiletries several times before I muster the courage to open the door and peep inside the bedroom.

The bathroom light casts a soft glow across the dark room and a light snore from the bed relaxes me. Confident that Aiden is safely asleep and no longer waltzing around half-naked like a man-sized piece of forbidden fruit, I creep over to the bed.

A flash of light stops me in my tracks, and I look down at my hand. The diamond ring catches the moonlight and shines so beautifully, I wonder if I'm actually asleep on the bathroom floor. The window is open a crack, and I close my eyes for a moment, listening to the steady tide rolling in and out. It's as if I can hear the Earth breathing.

Then, a yawn takes over my body and I ache in places I didn't know could ache. The sun will be up in a few hours, and I have to impress the Fitzgeralds. With that thought, I grab a stack of cushions and make a barrier in the middle of the bed. Then I curl up on the very edge of my side. But even though we're laying several feet apart, I can still sense Aiden's warmth, and nothing stops my stomach from squirming. Maybe I am getting sick? It's just like all the times I used to fake a migraine to get out of gym class and then ended up getting a real one.

Tomorrow, it's going to take all of my acting talent to pull this off. But there's no going back now. Aiden needs me, and I will not let him down.

CHAPTER 15

THERE IS ONE DESIGN FLAW IN THIS HOTEL:
white curtains. As soon as the sun rises, the
whole room is flooded with bright light. For a
few moments, I think I am having a heavenly
visitation from a messenger telling me to
change my ways. Maybe the Ghost of
Christmas Past works off season and I'll be
taken back to the bridal shop to see how
foolish I was.

But maybe the problem stems much
deeper than that? If I hadn't messed up my
pitch and lost my job, I wouldn't have been in
the bridal boutique. Or maybe I shouldn't
have made a deal with my boss to fire me if

the board didn't totally fall in love with the Schnooze shoes?

Although, if none of those things happened, I wouldn't be curling my hair at the dressing table of a five-star hotel in Hawaii right now. Is a vacation worth all that pain and hassle? The jury is still out. But what's done is done, and now I need to focus on Aiden's favor.

I pick a light floral halter-neck dress with a pair of strappy sandals. I need to look ravishing on Aiden's arm, he's a classy man. Almost always wearing a suit - when he's not walking around shirtless, that is - and has this old-fashioned manner about him. It's like he has an old soul. He loves listening to Frank Sinatra on his vintage record player, never fails to open a door for a woman, and he has this smile. It's a confident smile, but also bashful. And the way his eyes twinkle when he looks at me makes my knees...

"Should your hair be smoking?"

I jump in my seat and look at the reflection of Aiden in the mirror. "What?"

I had been so lost in thought, daydreaming about Aiden's twinkling eyes, I didn't notice that my hair is now stuck to the curling iron and indeed smoking. "NO!"

I gingerly unwrap the hair from the wand and pray it doesn't snap off. It falls into a tight ringlet by my cheekbone, warming my face. "Oh, thank goodness."

I turn back and take in Aiden's sand-colored dress pants and white cotton shirt. He's left the top two buttons undone and stands strong, with his shoulders squared and his hands in his pockets.

"You look handsome," I think aloud, my shoulders falling as I do my best to resist swooning. Aiden inclines his head and walks over to me. Then he takes a section of my dark hair and grazes his thumb over it.

"And you look exquisite," he murmurs, lowering to press his lips against my forehead. "Are you ready to go?"

Mr. and Mrs. Fitzgerald have their own private room for breakfast, it has a large window facing the sea. We're greeted by a middle-aged man with a neat beard and a tall blonde woman who looks like she just walked off a fashion runway in Paris. I take Aiden's arm, squeezing his tense bicep, and glance at him. He's nervous too.

"Well aren't you two a sight for sore eyes." Mr. Fitzgerald rises to his feet and greets me with a hug and a kiss on my cheek. The bristles of his beard scratch me.

"Mr. Fitzgerald, this is Emma, my fiancé," Aiden says as we break apart.

"Please. Call me Bill. Nice to meet you Emma. This is my wife, Jane." He gestures to the blonde who tenderly cradles my cheek.

"We've heard so much about you, please take a seat."

She gestures to the circular table, laden with fruit and pastries.

After we exchange pleasantries, Aiden strikes up a technical conversation, while Jane keeps her gaze steady on me as she cradles a steaming cup of coffee. It's unnerving.

"So, what do you do?" I ask her, in an attempt to steer her attention away from me. She sets her drink down and tilts her head, as if pondering the question.

"I'm a nurse at the Children's Hospital." Her words cut me, and my breath catches in my chest. Aiden and Bill stop talking and my stomach churns as Bill drapes his arm around his wife's shoulders.

"We think it's a mighty fine thing you two

are doing. Donating to the hospital. It's the very reason I chose to work with Aiden. It's the calibre of a man I look for to work in my company."

My face is on fire, as if I'm standing right in front of an open fire. Their eyes are like lasers, boring into my soul. Aiden wraps his arm around my waist, and I grip onto his hand for support. How are we going to pull this off? People are making donations to the hospital already, and thanks to the media attention, the numbers are rising.

Bill and Jane exchange looks before Bill takes his arm back and leans forward. "Jane works in the oncology department. This weekend is a much needed break for her, after many long shifts day in day out. And we wanted to invite you along to show our appreciation."

So that's why we're here? As a thank you for donating to the Children's Hospital.

"It's so nice to walk barefoot on the sand. Nursing shoes are practical, but nothing prevents the pain of being on your feet for twenty-hours."

I nod vacantly as a thought flickers like a lightbulb in my mind.

"You know, I'm a shoe designer, and I recently pitched a concept to solve that problem."

"Oh?"

I bite my lip and hold my breath for a moment, considering whether to explain. Aiden gives me a reassuring nod, and with that, I pull out my phone and scroll through the pictures.

"I call them the Schnooze shoes. They're a soft fluffy slipper on the inside... but a sensible work shoe on the outside. They offer maximum comfort while maintaining a professional image."

Jane hums with admiration as she scrolls through my pictures.

"That a fascinating concept. Did they like it?"

I grin sheepishly at her as she passes my phone back.

"They decided to go in another direction," I say carefully. Bill shakes his head with his brows knitted together.

"That's too bad. Sounds like a novel idea."

The conversation moves on, but I sit in silence, letting out the occasional noise of interest while I pick through the fruit on my plate. If only there was a shoe manufacturer who would listen to my idea.

"Why don't you two enjoy the resort for a few hours. We've booked a tour of the cave this afternoon. Bill will send you the details." Jane claps her hands as we all rise from the table. My stomach flips as we part ways and Aiden leads me back to our room, his fingers interlocking mine as he holds my hand.

"What do you say we get out of these clothes?" he asks. I gulp as my blood turns cold.

"What?"

A flush of color rises to his face as he coughs. "I mean, let's get into our swimwear. I want to take you to the beach."

I release my breath and nod along. A romantic stroll along the beach alone with Aiden on a tropical island? Sounds like just what the doctor ordered.

CHAPTER 16

The water is so warm as it laps at our ankles. Walking barefoot on the beach and leaving footprints in the sand is just as relaxing as it sounds. Aiden stoops down and splashes me, then wades further into the sea. I giggle like a high schooler and follow. The sky is crystal clear and the sunshine sparkles like diamonds on the surface of the water.

Aiden and I frolic and play like a couple of kids. Neither of us care what we might look like to the other people on the beach. He picks me up in his burly arms and wrestles me to the sandy floor. I roll over and splash him, and we both laugh and laugh.

Finally, we collapse on our beach towels,

chests heaving, and look up at the bright sky, waiting to catch our breath.

My heart is light, and I can't stop touching Aiden. Our hands are probably magnetized, it's the only logical reason we can't stop holding hands. As I lay on the beach, with the sun warming my skin and rushing waves calming my soul, I don't want to leave. If only this moment can last forever.

But a vibration jolts me out of my trance, and Aiden's hand slips away from mine. He rolls over and rummages through his pile of clothes.

"Everything okay?" I ask, propping myself up on my elbows. Aiden sighs, his back still turned. I trace the outline of his back muscles with my finger and circle the mole on his spine.

"My dad has been trying to call me."

He rolls back and drags his hands over his face with a huff.

Aiden doesn't talk about his parents much. I've never met them. All that Aiden would say about his family was that there are loads of them and everyone is loud and crazy. I find it difficult to picture Aiden coming from a big, loud family. He's introverted and I don't think I've ever heard him raise his voice.

"Why don't you call him back?" I ask. Aiden removes his hands to give me a look.

"My dad never calls. So, what do you think he's trying to talk to me about?"

I swallow hard. "Oh, right. The engagement."

I sit up and look away from him, watching the seagulls swooping from the sky to pester a bald man sunbathing in the distance.

"Who knew an innocent lie could spiral so much?" I muse aloud. "I didn't expect any of this to happen, you know. I only wanted to-"

Aiden takes my arm and I look back at him, meeting his intense stare. "You don't have to explain this to me. If I'm honest, I'm glad about how everything has turned out."

I laugh, but when Aiden doesn't laugh too, I cock a brow at him.

"You're serious?"

"Think about it. The Children's Hospital, my work, this trip… none of it would have happened if you told Shelly you were just having a bad day."

I chew my lip and look down, but Aiden

places his knuckle under my chin and tilts my head to meet his gaze again.

"Besides, we get to spend some time together alone."

He glances at my lips and I can hardly believe what's happening. Is Aiden Daniels coming onto me?

"I—I…" No more words come out of my lips as I flutter my lashes and try not to squeal with excitement. The setting is so perfect. I swallow and lick my dry lips, wondering if I have time to apply some Chapstick before he kisses me.

"Emma…" Aiden says, barely above a whisper. His face leans in closer, and his breath tickles my cheeks. I remain frozen, trying to stop the world from spinning and willing my stomach to stop doing flips. "I need to tell you something."

I want to act sultry and sweet, batting my lashes and murmuring "Go on," in a deep velvety voice. But instead, I sit immobile, eyes bulging like saucers. A tiny squeak comes out of my mouth. But before Aiden can share whatever it is he wants to tell me, a sudden splat knocks me out of my daze.

"You've got bird poop in your hair." The

words tumble out of me before I can stop them and my finger points at the white patch on the top of Aiden's head. His entire face turns crimson. "I've heard that's good luck," I add, trying to be helpful. In a beat, Aiden dashes into the sea and disappears beneath the water. Huge splashes ensue as if he's battling a white shark with his bare hands.

"Is it gone?" He asks, returning to me. Drops of water cling to his dark hair and every crevice of his perfectly sculpted body. I couldn't care less if he had five bird poops in his hair.

"What were you going to tell me?" I press, clutching his forearm. Aiden's cheeks flush but he marches off and picks up his belongings.

"It doesn't matter. We better go back and get ready. The tour starts in an hour." He avoids eye contact as he walks back up the beach towards the resort, and I begrudgingly follow, cursing the honking birds flying above.

CHAPTER 17

THE MURKY GREEN WATER ILLUMINATES THE cave in the most magical way. It's like we've stepped into another world and any moment now, a beautiful mermaid will appear from the depths.

"How deep is the water?" Bill asks the guide, who straightens his glasses and clears his throat.

"Deep enough to get lost down there. So, we do not allow diving."

"But we can take a dip?"

Swimming in cave water? That's a new experience. We remove our outer clothes and slide in. The water is ice-cold. Goosebumps begin to form on my skin. The cave is cool, as if fitted with its own natural type of air conditioning. I kick my legs to stay afloat and look down; the darkness below is unsettling. Aiden, however, is swimming around like a fish, completely undeterred. Jane dips one toe in and quickly moves away from the edge.

"I'll watch from here," she calls out, playing with her hair. Bill's roaring laugh echoes around the cave and he jumps in, causing a thunderous wave of water to drench both Jane and the guide. I stifle a laugh with my hands. Aiden chortles. The guide proceeds to talk about the history of the cave, and his voice floats over my head as I'm too interested in watching Aiden. His broad grin makes me weak at the knees. If I'm not careful, I might stop kicking my legs and slip down to the very bottom, never to see the light of day again. And when I make it to heaven, people will ask me how I died.

"Aiden smiled at me," is all I'll be able to say.

Suddenly, my leg makes contact with something and an agonizingly sharp pain rockets up my calf. The pain slams into my heart like a thunderbolt.

"I've been stung!" I shriek, flapping my

arms and flailing as Aiden launches to my side.

"Stung by what?" Bill doesn't wait for me to answer and returns to the edge.

"Jellyfish?" Jane asks the guide, who shrugs back.

"Highly unlikely," he shoots back. Aiden scoops me up in his arms and lifts me out of the water and Bill offers me his hand. My leg burns and the cool air does nothing to soothe it. Bill helps me onto the side, pulling me up with his rough hands, and I stagger to the cave wall, trying to get as far from the water as possible.

"Aiden, you'll have to pee on her leg."

"WHAT!" Aiden and I say at the same time. I had seen on TV shows that urine soothes a jellyfish sting. But up until now, I thought it was just a joke. Jane helps me to the ground and stretches out my leg to inspect it.

"Hold on... this isn't a sting." She looks up at the guide who stares in shock, clearly out of his depth. "Do you have a first aid kit?"

He nods silently as he takes out a kit from his backpack and hands it over. Jane makes no hesitation in getting to work patching me up.

Knowing I haven't been stung and will be

spared the eternal humiliation of getting peed on, I peek at my calf. Jane's right, it's not a sting. But it's a pretty big cut. The sight of blood makes my stomach churn. I look away and swallow against the excessive saliva building in my mouth. Aiden hurries to my side and takes my hand.

"Ah, yes. There are some jagged rocks in there. I suppose that's why they say no diving." Everyone glares at the guide, then turns their attention back to me. I'm not sure why drama follows me wherever I can go.

"I'm so sorry," I say, as Jane sanitizes the wound.

Bill has a word with the guide, but he's speaking too softly for me to hear. There's a look of terror on the guide's face, however, and that says a lot. Aiden squeezes my hand.

"Does she need stitches?"

"No, but you'll need to keep an eye on it. No more swimming until it's healed. Last thing you want is to have an infected wound on your wedding day." Jane pats my arm and my breath hitches as she presses a cotton pad on my wound. It throbs.

Aiden carries me out of the cave and all the way back to the shuttle bus waiting outside. Once we arrive back at the hotel, he insists on carrying me back to our room, and I can't say no.

He kicks the door open and lays me tenderly on the bed.

"How do you feel?"

"I'm okay. It's just sore."

"Bill and I were talking… he's had Francé Perrier cater for one of his events, and he said he wanted to book him for our wedding."

"No way."

"Yeah. Crazy, huh? When I told him I hadn't booked the Plaza hotel yet, he told me he would handle that too."

"Why is he being so nice?"

"Well, he's a high-profile person in the industry. I'm sure that his intentions are not entirely altruistic."

I lay back with my head on the plush pillow and close my eyes against the thumping headache creeping across my forehead. What a day.

"My mind is spinning, and I feel shaky. Do you think we can order food to the room?"

"Absolutely."

I listen to Aiden shuffle around the bed and pick up the phone receiver. "What do you want? I guess you should stay away from seafood."

I frown at the question until I remember last night, when I pretended to have food poisoning from shrimp.

"Good plan. Why don't you surprise me? You know what I like?"

Aiden's warm hand rests on my arm and I inhale deeply, relaxing further into the bed.

"Yes, I do," he said.

Listening to him talking in a low voice on the phone sends me off into a light sleep. Long minutes pass, and the mattress shifts with a squeak as Aiden settles back after finishing the call. He whispers something, but I'm stuck in the limbo between sleep and wakefulness to make out the words. I try to speak, but all that comes out of my mouth is a little moan.

"I was thinking…" Aiden says quietly. I'm not sure whether he's thinking aloud or talking to me. "What if we didn't call off the wedding?"

THE REST OF OUR TRIP PROVES UNEVENTFUL. I pretend not to have heard Aiden's musings, and he doesn't bring them up. Bill and Jane turn out to be pretty down to earth. That comes as a surprise to me.

Jane and I exchange numbers, and her parting words are about the wedding.

"I can't wait to see you in your dress! You're going to be a beautiful bride."

I grit my teeth and stay quiet during the entire flight, and Aiden does not press me to have a conversation. The deep crease between his brows and puckered lips tells me he's stuck inside his own thoughts too.

As we return to our apartment block, Aiden steals a glance at me and holds out his hand. I take it without hesitation and his grazes my diamond ring with his thumb.

"Well, job done," I say lightly. Aiden searches my eyes with a frown as I slide the ring off my finger and hold it out for him. "I guess you need this back."

Aiden opens his mouth, but the elevator pings and he breaks eye contact.

"Dad!"

A rush of adrenaline jolts my heart as I force the ring back on my finger and turn to the middle-aged man standing in front of the elevator. Apart from a slimmer frame and greying hair, he looks just like his son.

He pulls Aiden into a hug before turning to me, his grey eyes flicker to my hand and a huge grin spreads across his face. Before I can utter a word, he plants a kiss on my cheek and scoops me up in the tightest hug I've ever had.

"We're all excited Aiden has finally asked you-"

"Dad, is everything okay? What are you doing here?" Aiden interrupts, a hint of panic in his voice. Aiden's dad lets me go and claps his hand on Aiden's shoulder.

"You've not been returning my calls; your mother is worried you two are going to elope."

Aiden and I exchange looks.

"Don't tell me you've already done it?" Aiden's dad says, taking a step back.

"No dad, you didn't miss anything. We've been away."

"Hawaii," I add, as if that's any help. Aiden's dad looks from Aiden to me, before looking back at his son again with wide eyes.

"Hawaii? It's a tad early for a honeymoon, don't you think?"

Aiden and I start talking at the same time,

our voices jumble together as we wave our hands.

"No, no, no," I say in a voice so deep; it doesn't sound like my own. The corners of the man's eyes crease as he watches us with amusement.

"Well, anyway…" he clears his throat. "Your mother and I have arranged a dinner with Emma's parents."

"You have?" I blurt, my blood turning cold.

"Dad, you didn't have to-"

"Your mother insists. Now, tomorrow night, we'd love to see you both there."

"Right, but it's just us?" Aiden says, eyeing his dad with hope.

"-and the family."

Aiden's face grows pale. "The family? You invited the whole family?"

Aiden swivels his head and looks at me ashen faced, as if I have just been signed up to participate in a battle to the death.

"See you tomorrow night, seven sharp."

Aiden's dad returns to the elevator and we wave weakly as the doors close again. Now alone, I grab Aiden's arm.

"Our families are having dinner together. Do you realize what this is?"

"A nightmare."

"We're in too deep. I can't see how we can get out of this."

Aiden's words from last night repeat in my head as I chew my lip.

"Would it be so bad... to just go along with the wedding?"

Aiden looks at me like I've just suggested the moon is a donut. Speaking of... I would kill for a glazed ring donut right now.

"You want to get married? For real?" Aiden asks, his bushy brows raising.

"Hey, don't look at me like that. What choice do we have? The Fitzgerald's have got involved with the wedding planning; our families are getting to know each other. Don't forget the Children's Hospital."

Aiden nods along, looking at the floor.

"It's just... not what I had pictured."

"Look... we can get an annulment afterward. No one would have to find out. And you keep your client, the hospital gets their scanning equipment, our families get to see us marry. Everyone wins."

Aiden's eyes are sorrowful as he studies me.

"Are you sure you want to do this? I mean, you're going to meet my whole family tomorrow. And we have to convince them we're real."

"Yes," I say with as much confidence as I can muster. "We just... have to pretend we're head over heels in love right? How hard can that be?" I chuckle to myself, but Aiden cradles my cheek and his eyes moisten as he looks at me deeply.

"I wish..." he breaks off. Then he bends down and presses his lips against my forehead.

"Hey, it'll be fine." I squeeze his hand. "We've got this."

CHAPTER 18

I HAVEN'T GOT THIS.

Aiden and I walk up to the large suburban home, hand in hand. They set a hog roast and tables laden with food up on the front lawn under a marquee.

This is not a quiet dinner. I had pictured a large table with maybe twenty adults, listening to Bing Crosby and complimenting Aiden's mom on her cooking.

Instead, everyone is out on the lawn, with at least twenty children darting in and out of the house, screeching at the top of their lungs. The sound of a new-born baby's cry cuts through everything else like a dagger, straight to my heart.

"This is your family?" I side glance at Aiden and he squeezes my hand. Then he let's go so he can wrap his arm around my waist.

"They're here!" A tall brunette woman, with eyes shaped just like Aiden's, approaches. Her black dress reaches the floor and glitters in the lamplights.

"Mom, this is Emma."

"I know who you are, welcome to the family."

She throws her arms around me and a waft of her perfume washes over my senses. When we break apart, she claims my face with her hands and gives me a piercing look.

"I'm so happy my baby has found such a beautiful, smart, young woman." A twinge of guilt nips at my insides as she lets me go to kiss Aiden on the cheek. "Come on, meet the rest of the family."

Aiden has five sisters and a brother. All of them are older than him. I am introduced to Harper first, the oldest of the clan. She has six children under the age of nine, manages her own YouTube channel for parenting, and is married to Oscar, a life coach from Illinois. She points her kids out in the crowd and hands me a plate of cornbread.

"Everyone helps out in this family. Find a place on the table for these, will you?"

Aiden picks up a plate of rolls and walks with me to the marquee.

"Harper is the bossy one," he mutters. I give him a wry look, but then we bump into a short, young woman, who cannot be older than twenty. She has rich brown hair and narrow features.

"This is Isabella," Aiden says warmly as he sets down the plate and gives his sister a hug. "She's an artist."

"Oh please," she says with a scoff. "You have to actually sell your work to be an artist. I work in a grocery store."

"What kind of art do you make?" I ask, curious.

"Clowns."

I gulp. "Clowns? As in…"

"Creepy, hide under your bed, murderous clowns? Yeah, those clowns," she says, her voice low. There's an awkward moment where I'm not sure what to say but merely blink at her. Then Aiden's laugh breaks the ice.

"Bella… Emma doesn't know your dark sense of humor." He turns to me. "She's joking."

"Sorry," Isabella says quickly, her face breaking into a delighted smile. "I just love the reaction I get when I say that." She pulls out her phone and thrusts it at my face. "This is what I make."

She scrolls through endless pictures of landscapes and not one picture of a clown appears, much to my relief.

"You're so talented."

Aiden moves me through the crowd of people, introducing me to cousins, uncles… he wasn't joking when he said I'd be meeting the whole family.

"Emma, your parents are here," Aiden says, nodding in the direction of the street. My parents walk up, arm in arm, with identical expressions of terror. I'm an only child. The biggest family reunion we've ever been to was at Great Aunt Margaret's retirement party. There were twelve guests. That's it.

"Look out everyone, we are in the presence of royalty. The kings have arrived!" Aiden's dad shouts. The babble of talk quietens as Aiden buries his face with his hands.

My parents look baffled as they wander toward us. I rush out to meet them and pull them both in for a group hug. Never have I ever been so happy to see them.

"I'm so sorry, my family is…" Aiden begins, but his parents reach them before he can finish.

"Welcome to our home. It's wonderful to have you join us."

"It's nice to meet… all… of Aiden's family," my mom says, glancing at the sea of eyes all pointed at us. "I'm sorry, if I'd known… I would have brought more food." She hands Aiden's mom a cake.

"Don't be silly. Come on in and meet the rest of us," Aiden's mom leads my parents to the party and begins the introductions.

Aiden was right. His family is crazy. They sing karaoke, the kids are unruly, running around everywhere, and I'm introduced to so many people, my head starts spinning. Everyone has a dark, witty sense of humor. I hold onto Aiden's arm for dear life, grinning like a fool.

"How did you propose Aiden?" his brother asks.

"Oh, great idea. Everyone shut up, Aiden's going to tell us how he proposed to Emma," someone shouts from the back.

The marquee grows quiet as all eyes are on us. I clutch Aiden's arm and glance at him, but to my surprise, he's calm. He looks down for a moment, and a small smile crosses his face, then he looks up and clears his throat. Even the children stop playing and stare.

"Emma really loves donuts, and old movies," he begins. I muster my best impression of an all-knowing expression. Like I've heard this story a million times. But honestly, I'm not sure where he's going with this.

"So, there's this old movie theatre just outside the city. They have a break in the middle of the movie when people can buy ice cream and snacks."

A collective sigh fills the air at the same time as the men roll their eyes.

"I took Emma to watch Gone with the Wind."

"That's my all-time favorite movie!" I blurt. Aiden looks at me with a chuckle.

"Yes dear, that's why I took you, remember?" He nudges me with his elbow, and I clamp my lips together with a nod. Aiden turns back to the crowd of people hanging onto his every word. "We were wearing our best clothes; she had this long red dress on…"

Someone wolf whistles.

"Anyway, during the intermission, I offered to buy some snacks. But I had already arranged with the owners of the theatre to make the move."

Excitement is reaching fever pitch and I hold my breath, captivated by his words.

"Everyone stayed in their seats, while the lights dimmed again, and a single spotlight hovered on this beautiful woman. The look on her face when I got down on one knee, holding out a Krispy crème donut..."

"Like that one!" someone shouts. My mouth is hanging open. I recover myself with a sheepish grin and tuck a stray hair behind my ear.

"The screen lit up with the words 'Emma King, will you marry me?' and in the middle of the donut was the ring."

The whole party swoons. Even the men seem caught up in the story.

"And what did you do, Emma?" My dad asks, prompting other people to urge me on. Emotion catches in my chest and I'm not sure I can speak. I turn to Aiden and look up into his eyes for courage.

"I was so shocked. It was the last thing I

expected him to do," I begin. "We've gone to that movie theatre together every month for years." It's not a lie. Ever since he told me he was into the classics; we would go and watch one together at the Curzon. It's a small, family run theatre from the 1950's. Everything he said is true. Apart from the proposal, of course. But I can see it so clearly in my head, for all I know, it did happen, and I had forgotten until now.

"What did you say?" one of Aiden's sisters shouted.

"Isn't that part obvious?" a male remarked, prompting laughter.

"I want to hear it," the sister retorted.

I bite my lip to steady my nerves then beam at the crowd, my hands holding Aiden's.

"I said, 'Yes, of course I will,' then he kissed me, and it was just like the end of an old movie."

The marquee erupts into applause.

"Show us, Aiden. Kiss her!"

I look back at Aiden, my pulse racing. But he doesn't hesitate. He takes his hands from mine and tenderly cradles my face. My breath hitches as he stoops down and his nose nuzzles my cheek as his lips brush against mine. My foot pops in the air and I cling onto his back as we share our very first - fake - kiss. But there's absolutely nothing fake about it. As he moves his lips over mine, my body zings and I rise on my tip toes to greedily take more of him. His hands leave my heated cheeks and he grasps my waist, lifting me in the air.

The cheers and clapping are distant over the thump of my heartbeat, and the sudden drumming in my ears. Aiden spins me in a circle and finishes the kiss with several chaste pecks on my cheeks. He lowers me to the ground again and we break apart, grinning like fools.

"Here's to Aiden and Emma… and true love!"

Everyone cheers again, and the moment ends. The music starts up, karaoke resumes, and the children gleefully continue their game. But for me, everything has stopped. Aiden takes my hand and leads me toward the drive. Now alone, he pulls me in for a hug.

"Emma… that was…" He breaks off and buries his face in my neck. Puffs of air from his nostrils tickle me and I squirm away with a laugh.

"I know," I say through a breath. "How

did you think up that story so fast? I mean… it was perfect. No one suspects a thing."

Aiden lifts my hand and eyes the sparkling diamond with a knowing smile.

"It just came to me," he said. Then his face grows serious. "This is really happening, isn't it?"

I trace a line from his furrowed brow to his defined cheekbone and down to his chin. Then I sigh. My body, still tingling, is so light and happy, any minute now, I'll surely float up into the sky. I pinch myself hard and my eyes moisten at the pain.

"We're not dreaming, if that's what you mean."

As if to check I'm real, Aiden squeezes my arms, then my waist, and settles his hands on my cheeks as he looks deeply into my eyes. We stand in silence for a few minutes, just looking at each other as if for the very first time. Then he plants another kiss on my lips, so warm and gentle it's like coming home after a long day at work. He kisses me again, even though no one from the party is watching. Finally, he lets me go and his eyes twinkle in the streetlamps.

"Good," he says in a low voice.

CHAPTER 19

THE LINE BETWEEN MAKE-BELIEVE AND REALITY
is blurred. The next two months pass by in a
beautiful whirlwind. Like a cheesy montage in
a movie. I land a new job, thanks to the exten-
sive portfolio Katie put together for me. Of
course, no one wants to hear about my shoe
designs yet, but it's early days.

Aiden and I spend almost all our spare
time together. We hold hands, even when no
one is around. I've become so accustomed to
it, not holding hands with him feels wrong. My
mom and Aiden's mom have become best
friends. They make all the arrangements for
the big day, much to my relief. Wedding plan-

ning is not fun. Nor is it as glamorous as it looks on TV.

Except for the day they take me to Noelle's and make me try on the dress I always dreamed of owning. Aiden's mom and my mom cling to each other, teary-eyed and sighing as I twirl on the spot.

"You look breath-taking," my mom says with a sniff. Aiden's mom nods. "Aiden is a very lucky man."

The moment is just as magical as I imagine it to be.

Now, my Vera Wang dress hangs in my closet, and my count down calendar only has one more day to tick off before the wedding.

But when Aiden and I arrive at the Plaza to go over the plans, I can't ignore the sickly feeling in my stomach. Things between us feel so right, so why does this wedding feel so wrong?

"I can't believe we're getting married here," I whisper to him as the guide takes us to our room. Rows of seats sit pretty with pastel pink organza bows fastened to the ends of the aisle. A harp sits in the corner. Pink rose petals run up to the front. My heart flutters at the sight of everything set up, ready and waiting for the special day.

Thanks to all the media attention, the Children's Hospital has received enough donations to reopen a wing that closed down for renovation nearly a decade ago.

Bill Fitzgerald promises to match whatever donations we raise. His face is on every major paper in the city because of it. Which does make me question why he didn't donate to the hospital in the first place, if he's so rich and his wife works there. Maybe Aiden is right and it's less about altruism and more about his reputation. I shake the thoughts away.

As we walk out into the entrance hall, I notice Shelly standing to the side, wiping her eyes with her hands. Frederick is nowhere to be seen. With a frown, I break away from Aiden's hold and walk over to her.

"Shelly... are you okay?" I ask.

"Oh, yes. I'm fine." She hiccups and sniffs as more tears leak out of her eyes. I cannot help but notice her puckered lips look even more swollen than usual.

Aiden takes out a handkerchief and offers it to her. She looks at him with mild alarm, then her bottom lip quivers and she snatches it from him with a wail.

"The wedding is off!" She sobs into her hands and blows her nose in the handkerchief with ferocity. The sound echoes around the entire hall.

Aiden steps back, probably sensing an awkward conversation he has no interest being party to.

"Do you want to call the caterers?" I whisper to him. Aiden nods gratefully, and leaves.

After checking that there is no one else around to be a support, I lead Shelly to a row of chairs by the front door to offer us more privacy. In all the years we were at school together, I never saw Shelly cry. I'm not sure what to do. But leaving her in this sorry state is not an option.

"The truth is… Frederick and me… We're not…" she breaks off and looks away from me.

"Not what?" I ask, puzzled.

Shelly closes her eyes and takes a deep breath.

"He's Canadian, and if he doesn't marry an American, they're going to have him deported," she says in one breath. I resist the urge to gasp.

"Wait, he's marrying you for a marriage visa?"

"To be perfectly honest, I can't stand the guy," Shelly says, her voice regaining strength. She avoids my gaze with a frown and looks at the marble floor.

"But what about Africa?" I ask, mystified.

Shelly smirks before looking at me again.

"All fake. Backdrops. Neither of us have even been to Africa."

Well, that makes more sense. The thought of Shelly running a vaccination program is just as far-fetched as the idea of me meeting the love of my life in London.

"But I don't understand, what do you get out of it?" I ask, not able to connect the dots.

"I thought I could show my followers what a glamorous life I have. You don't understand the pressure that comes with a big social media following. I mean Emma, it's my job."

"You're an influencer?"

"Exactly. So, he plays husband, and we work together to maintain…"

"…a lie?" I finish for her. I've never been

interested in social media, maintaining a fake lifestyle sounds exhausting.

"Only thing is, someone recognized Frederick and blew the whistle. Now the wedding is off, Frederick has gone back to Canada and I've lost over ten thousand followers. My life is over." She buries her face in her hands and her shoulders shake violently. I nervously pat her back, wondering what to do.

"Gosh, I'm so sorry. I thought you two were annoyingly perfect, but I never doubted you were the real deal."

"Not like you and Aiden." Shelly lifts her head and sniffs as she looks at me.

I frown back at her. "What do you mean?"

"Seeing as I'm being so honest, I thought you were feeding me a bunch of lies back at the boutique." She flicks her hair back and chuckles, as if laughing at a secret joke.

"You did?"

"And to be honest, I wanted to see you squirm. So, I posted about your wedding online. Made it go viral. But then you and Aiden showed up to my engagement party and completely stole the show. You two were all that anyone could talk about."

"Shelly, I am so…" I can't bring myself to

finish the sentence. At least, not to tell another lie. Part of me is furious that she had an agenda to hurt me. Yet, I should have seen it coming. It is so like Shelly to do something like this.

As if reading my mind, she waves a hand aside with a sigh. "Forget it. I brought this on myself. If I didn't make those posts about you, no one would know who you are."

It's the closest to an apology I'll ever get from her.

"Well, it's thanks to you that the Children's Hospital has been raking it in."

We both laugh. Then I lean forward, rest my elbows on my knees and sigh. "I'm sorry about you and Frederick."

"It is what it is. I was being delusional, thinking we could make it work. A relationship that's based on a lie... it never works. As they say, the truth always comes out."

Her words make my blood turn cold.

"Shelly. I have to tell you something."

"You were just trying on wedding dresses for fun? I know."

"HOW?" I sit bolt upright and gawp at her devilish grin.

"Emma. You seem to forget that I know

you. I can always tell when you're lying. I mean, Pandas in Bora Bora? Oh, please. Besides, doing something pathetic like trying on wedding dresses when you don't even have a boyfriend is totally the type of thing you'd do."

A rush of annoyance makes me grit my teeth.

"Then why didn't you tell me?"

"Honestly, I was curious about how far it would go. Then my Aunt Lizzie got involved and it became this big competition. She's always been jealous of your mom, so it became about her more than me."

She looks around the hall with a sigh.

"Lizzie, jealous of my mom? Now that is a revelation," I say through a breath.

"Are you kidding? Your parents have been married for what? Thirty years? She's on her third husband and even that one is on the rocks."

"Wow. I had no idea."

"I guess keeping up appearances is a trait that runs in my family. So, are you going ahead with it?"

I look down at my ring and chew my lip. For me, it hasn't been about keeping up appearances. Not since the party at Aiden's parents' house. But Shelly is right... this marriage is built on a lie. A big one.

"Are you going to call me out?"

The corners of Shelly's lips curve upward, but she shakes her head.

"I think I've done enough damage to other people's lives. Don't you?" She huffs, as if that took every ounce of her energy to say. "I guess I'm just a terrible person."

I pull her in for a hug.

"You're not terrible," I say finally. Suddenly, everything falls into place. Shelly, Lizzie... me... we all lie because of our own insecurities. But underneath the mask is a woman who is just trying not to humiliate herself. I never thought the day would come that I could understand. But here it is.

Shelly pulls away. "Does this mean you've forgiven me for kissing your boyfriend on graduation?"

I shrug. That was a million years ago. "Well, he kissed back, so he's just as guilty."

"For what it's worth, it was a terrible kiss." Shelly stifles a laugh with her hand as I give her a knowing look.

"Garlic breath?"

"Yes!"

I snort. "He swore his garlic supplements were odourless. But…"

We both laugh.

"There's something I've not been able to figure out… How did you find someone to agree to marry you so quickly?"

"Aiden is my best friend. We agreed to help each other out, and everything spiralled. Now… our 'lie' has become our reality. At least… it has for me."

"Well, I hope you two figure things out. You're cute together. And he's…" she picks up the soiled handkerchief and eyes it with furrowed brows, "Just as quirky as you."

"What are you going to do now?" I ask her, quickly changing the subject as Aiden approaches us.

Shelly sighs, her shoulders slumping. "Well, I'm going to try authenticity. Start up a new social media channel and post about real things."

We share a mutual smile.

Aiden returns to my side. "Are you ready to go?"

I look up at him, my heart squeezing so tightly, I can barely breathe. To start a marriage like this is wrong, but I'm not sure I have the strength to do what I have to do to make it right.

"Not yet. I need to make a quick call. Then, we need to talk."

CHAPTER 20

SNAKES WRITHE IN MY STOMACH AS I WATCH the line of cars pull up outside the Plaza. My mom finishes fixing my hair and looks at me with alarm, but I shake my head at her. She promised not to say anything, and her lips are pursed so tightly, small lines appear around them.

"Here's the dress!" Katie says brightly, as she enters the dressing room. I turn from the window and study my best friend, my heart softening.

Katie had spent most of her time helping Colin's grandma. When she did return to the apartment, she was insistent on talking to me about my wedding. But a week ago, Colin appeared on the doorstep, wearing his military uniform. I should have left the room to give them privacy, but their reunion was too cute to walk away from. She flung herself into his arms and he caught her, spinning her round in a circle and kissing her face thousands of times.

"I left the military. I can't do this anymore. I want to marry you and be here for you, every day. For the rest of our lives."

Colin and Katie's love is real, and despite having very little money between them, they are happy. It makes what I have to do a little easier.

I nod to my mom, who looks deflated as she leaves the room.

"Katie, you're not wearing that, are you?" I say, trying to lace my words with disdain. Katie looks down at her rose-colored dress with a frown.

"You chose this dress," she points out, resting her hands on her hips. I chuckle as I stride across the room and pick up the Vera Wang from the chair.

"Good thing we're the same size. Now take it off. We need to get you ready."

"I don't understand… What's happening?"

I squeeze her shoulders and bite back tears. "This is your day now." The words come out in a whisper. Katie shakes her head, confused.

"What? It's your wedding day," she argues. I roll my lips inward and clamp my teeth as my vision is blurred by my tears.

"You are the most honest, selfless person I know. What you and Colin have is magical. And I want you to have this day because you deserve the best of the best. Besides, there is a handsome, ex-military man waiting for you to walk down the aisle. That is… if you'll still have him?"

Katie's eyes pool with tears as she gasps. "You arranged this? For me? But what about Aiden? I don't understand."

I dab under her eyes with a tissue and give her a hard look. "It's not about me, today it's about you. And we need to get you ready."

———

WALKING UP THE AISLE SEEMS TO TAKE AN age. Whispers fly around the room as the seated guests watch me. Aiden joins my side as I turn and face the guests. Time to tell the truth.

"We're here today, because of a stupid lie I told a few months ago." Aiden gives me a hollow look as he takes my hand.

When I told him my plan last night, he promised to help me put it into action.

"Aiden is my friend. And he agreed to go along with it. Because that's who he is. He'll do anything for anyone. I am sorry, but I can't go through with this wedding, because it would be a lie." I glance at Aiden apologetically as he pulls his hand away from mine. The hurt in his eyes is enough to break my heart a thousand times. I'm not sure if this is part of the act, or if he's truly hurt.

I tear myself away from him and look back at the horrified guests.

"I was pretending to be in love with him. It was just… an act. And a marriage that comes from a lie, is doomed. I know I will never be able to make it right. Or heal the pain I've caused. But there is one small thing I can do. So, there will be a wedding today."

I nod to the men standing beside the doors. They pull them open. The bewildered guests whisper to each other as they turn in their seats to find Colin walking up the aisle, dressed in a dark suit with a sheepish grin on his face.

Aiden strides to the back as I take my position at the front, holding a small bouquet. I smooth out the red skirt of my dress and put on my best smile as the doors open again. This time, the string quartet jump into action and follow the harpist, playing the most beautiful music.

Katie appears, with Aiden on her arm. The Vera Wang takes up the entire aisle as they walk to the front. The bewildered guests gasp. I smile at Colin's family; his grandma dabs her eyes with a tissue as she watches Katie join Colin. The two of them look like a prince and princess.

"Dearly beloved, we are gathered here today, to witness the marriage of Colin Masters, and Katie Griffith…"

Aiden avoids eye contact with me during the ceremony. And as soon as the reception is over, he leaves with his family asking him thousands of questions.

Katie does not have a family, she grew up in foster care and never imagined she would have a huge wedding like this. As they take their first dance, Colin's grandma pats my cheek with a twinkle in her eye.

"It was a brave thing you did back there."

My eyes pool with tears, obscuring the old lady from my vision as I smile back.

"I hurt a lot of people. But at least I could do this for Katie and Colin."

"What you did was a gift. I didn't know if I would live to see my grandson marry. And Katie is a wonderful girl. We have grown rather close these past months. Thank you."

There are so many unanswered questions. What will happen to the donations? Will people demand their money back? Will my parents look at me differently for the rest of my life? Will Aiden forgive me?

But as I watch Katie and Colin dancing in the middle of the round circle tables, my heart swells. This is not my happy ever after, it's theirs.

CHAPTER 21

KATIE MOVED OUT TO LIVE WITH HER NEW husband in New Jersey, and Aiden buried himself with work. Over the next month, I try to make plans with him, but he always has an excuse not to hang out with me. The apartment is quiet and still, and I cannot work out why I feel so hollow after doing something right.

Just as I replay the events of the wedding in my mind for the millionth time, the doorbell rings. I have visions of Aiden standing at my door with a bouquet of red roses as I leap off the couch and swing it open.

"I dooooo!"

A rush of heat floods my face as I throw

my hands over my mouth. Aiden is not standing at my door, professing his love for me.

Instead, Jane Fitzgerald faces me, with a puzzled look on her face.

"Sorry, I thought you were someone else," I say. "Come on in."

"Actually, I was hoping you could come with me. Have you heard of Lawrence and Jones?"

I shake my head.

"Well, they manufacture clothing and shoes specifically for medical staff."

"Right."

"I couldn't stop thinking about your Schnooze shoes and I got talking to the other nurses about it, and we all think it's an amazing concept. Are you free right now?"

I glance at the tissues littering my coffee table and the half-eaten tub of ice cream sitting on the armchair.

"I could reschedule some things," I say, trying to act aloof. "What did you have in mind?"

"I've got you ten minutes with a board of directors. But we have to be quick."

Shaken, I dash to pick up my prototype

shoes and a jacket and follow Jane out of the apartment.

"I can't believe this. I thought you must hate my guts after... everything." Jane stops and look at me frankly.

"Listen, I don't know what's going on between you and Aiden. But the chemistry between you two in Hawaii was undeniable. Honey, you can't fake love. And the way he looks at you... it's the real deal. Besides, what you did... giving your wedding away to your friend? Bill and I were so impressed. Aiden told us everything, and that takes unbelievable courage."

I glance at Aiden's door with a heavy sigh.

"That might be true. But he's barely talked to me since the wedding."

Jane plants a hand on my shoulder and gives it a squeeze.

"Don't give up. But right now, it's your time to show these people your design."

———

"WE'LL NEED TO HAVE YOU ONBOARD TO WORK with our designers on these. Obviously, there are some flaws to the concept that need to be

worked on. Functionality, support, breatha-
bility for example. But I like it."

I bite against a squeal. "You do?"

One of the men at the board gives me a
broad smile.

"I don't know why no one has done it
before now. So many people work many hours
on their feet every day. These can be game
changers in the market."

"Right," I nod along, grinning back. "I
can design all sorts of shoes."

I glance at Jane who gives me a thumbs up
from the door.

"Right. Then it's settled. We'll set up a
proper meeting to go through the particulars.
Thank you, Jane. Please thank Bill for
bringing this to my attention."

I'm on cloud nine. I have never under-
stood what was so special about cloud nine,
but I'm on it. I float out of the office building
with a goofy grin on my face.

"AIDEN OPEN UP. I NEED TO TALK TO YOU." I
bang on his door with my fist, refusing to
leave. I'll stand here all night if that's what it

takes. Thankfully, the door swings open after only a few minutes.

"Oh, hey Emma." Aiden's gaze does not quite meet mine as he crosses his arms and leans against his doorway. The dark rings under his eyes are new and his usually neat hair is ruffled.

"I got a deal. There's a company who wants to make my shoes." I throw myself at him and give him the tightest hug I can muster. He stiffens but hugs me back.

"That's great. I'm really happy for you."

As we break apart, I take a deep breath. "Listen, about the wedding…"

"Don't." Aiden looks at me properly this time and it hits me in the chest like a fiery poker stick.

"I didn't realize I hurt you so much, I mean we discussed it the night before and you seemed to be okay with it."

"Giving the wedding to Katie and Colin… is the nicest thing you've ever done for anyone. It was absolutely the right thing to do. I have no regrets." Aiden jerks his head and clears his throat, sounding official.

"Then why haven't we…" I break off,

overcome with emotion. I reach for his hand but he moves away. "I miss you."

Aiden's eyes moisten, but he doesn't speak.

"If you have no regrets, then what's wrong? I thought you'd be proud of me for finally coming clean and not pretending anymore?"

"That's just it," Aiden whispers. "I didn't realize you were just pretending. I thought what we had between us..."

I take a deep breath. His words weigh heavy on my chest.

"You love me?"

The question hangs in the space between us for a breath. Aiden unfolds his arms and rubs the back of his neck. Then he eyes me with a sincere look.

"Always have."

I don't know whether to laugh or cry.

"All this time, I thought it was just me. But I didn't want to jeopardize-"

"-Our friendship?" Aiden takes a step forward and picks up my hand, his eyes softening. I hold my breath.

"When I got the news about this company wanting to work with me, you know the first person I wanted to call?"

Aiden doesn't answer, and I raise my hand to his cheek. "You, Aiden. You're my person, the one I think about when I want to share… anything. It's always been you."

Aiden envelopes my body in his arms and I bury my face in his chest. His rapid heartbeat thumps against my ear, bringing a smile to my lips. Then he pulls back enough to look into my eyes again.

"May I take you on a date?" he asks softly. "There's a matinee of My Fair Lady tomorrow afternoon."

I grin like a Cheshire Cat and bob my head as my entire body buzzes.

Then, without another thought, I rise to the tip of my toes and kiss him chastely on the lips. Aiden wraps me in a bear hug and lifts me up from the ground. He grins at me when we break apart slightly.

"I'm taking that as a yes, then."

EPILOGUE

WHEN I WAS A LITTLE GIRL, I ALWAYS pictured a grand wedding for myself. A massive dress, hundreds of guests, a massive pile of presents and a cake the size of a Great Dane.

But my experiences have made me realize I don't want any of it.

Aiden proposed to me just one month after our official date. He played out the entire scenario he told his family at our fake engagement party.

Neither of us could cope with planning another wedding. So, we skipped all the formalities and set it for a workday, so only our closest family could be there. And I found a cute little chapel outside the city.

There are no photographers, white doves, caviar or famous caterers. I'm wearing a simple white gown, which has a lace overlay. But the way Aiden looks at me as I walk down the aisle makes me feel like a million dollars.

My dad kisses me on the cheek just before he hands me over to my husband-to-be, and whispers in my ear.

"Proud of you."

As the pastor announces us husband and wife, Aiden pulls me in for a kiss and my foot pops in the air. Music plays and the chapel rouses in applause.

At the reception, Aiden's family enjoys taking turns to give a toast. The room explodes with laughter at each one. His nieces and nephews keep tapping their glasses with spoons to make everyone chant "kiss, kiss, kiss."

The reception is messy and loud and anything but refined. Yet, it's oddly perfect.

As we take our first dance, the lights dim, and the room quietens enough to hear Frank Sinatra playing on the sound system. Aiden strokes my hair away from my face and nuzzles me softly before he spins me in a circle and recaptures me in his arms.

"I have a secret to share with you," he whispers in my ear as we dance cheek to cheek.

"Oh? What is that?"

"That ring I gave you?"

I run my thumb along the band as I listen.

"I bought it for you a year ago. I was just trying to build up the courage to make a move."

I pull back to look at him.

"You knew you wanted to marry me?"

"Of course. You're my best friend. I can't imagine living my life without you in it by my side."

I rest my head on his chest as we circle the spot.

"Promise me something," he whispers. I lift my head and stop dancing for a moment.

"Anything," I say with fervor. Aiden clutches my waist.

"Promise me we'll never lie to each other, or anyone else."

I laugh. "Oh, that's easy." Then, struck by a thought, I add, "Actually, Katie is going to an antenatal class next month, it's just for expectant parents. I was wondering maybe we could pretend…"

"NO."

I snort at Aiden's look of terror and place my hand in his as we dance again. "Just kidding."

THE END.

Author Note: *If you enjoyed this story, it would mean so much to me if you could leave a review.*

Keep reading for a sneak peek of the prequel to the Truth or Dare romcom series: What I Don't Like About You!

Want to read more romantic comedy?
Pick up your FREE copy of *Matched with a Billionaire* by signing up for Laura Burton's VIP newsletter here:

HTTPS://BOOKHIP.COM/VGDSML

ROMANTIC COMEDIES

Love comedy?

Here's the list of Laura Burton's laugh out loud romcoms.

Truth or Dare Romantic Comedy Series

What I Don't Like About You — Prequel

Dare Number One: Kiss Me Like You Mean It

Dare Number Two: Don't Fall in Love

Dare Number Three: Pretend to be Mine

Love Me, Romcom

Love Me in the Spotlight

Love Me Like You Mean It

Love Me I'm Your Princess

BILLIONAIRES

Here is the list of titles and the order to read them for the best experience.

Billionaires in New York

Matched with a Billionaire—Prequel

(Grab your copy here! https://bookhip.com/VGDSML)

Who Wants to Love a Billionaire? (Book 1)

Who Wants to Kiss a Billionaire? (Book 2)

Who Wants to Date a Billionaire? (Book 3)

Billionaires in Los Angeles

How to Tame a Billionaire Cowboy (Book 1)

How to Nanny a Billionaire's Baby (Book 2)

How to Fire Your Billionaire Boss (Book 3)

PREVIEW OF WHAT I DON'T LIKE ABOUT YOU

Debbie

NOTE TO SELF: CONSUMING EXCESSIVE amounts of sugar is just as bad as drinking too much alcohol. *This* is why I don't go to parties. Everyone knows I'm much happier at my tiny apartment in upstate New York, curled up with a snuggly blanket, breaking the spine of a new book and tearing through the pages like a literary monster.

In fact, right now I'd rather be at my local DIY store looking at thirty-two different shades of white than sit in Michelle's living room with all of these people.

I don't mean to be a Debbie-downer. Though, my name actually *is* Debbie. But parties make me uncomfortable. Especially in a suburban home in New Jersey. With twitchy neighbors and uptight locals with the cops on speed dial.

Besides, parties often involve too many people, deafening music blasting my ear drums, and nothing but junk food in sight.

So, what do I do? I down sugar shots like I'm twelve years old because I do not drink, and the sugar rush has me bouncing off the walls.

"Debbie Brown. It's my twenty-first birthday, and you're my best friend. You *have* to come to my party," Michelle said, giving me her puppy-dog eyes. Michelle and I have been friends since we were in diapers. In fact, as I look around the cramped living room at the sea of faces, I realize there isn't a soul in this house who isn't a close friend.

Cameron and Jonah have been part of the group since our first year in college when Michelle made me join the Glee Club. Holly and Katia have been our roommates since our second year. And then there's Ryder. He looks as awkward and disgruntled as I feel.

But now the sugar is rushing to my head and my brain is full of bees.

"Where are you going?" Michelle asks, her big round eyes fixed on me as I rise to my feet.

"I'm going to use the bathroom. Is that okay with you?" I ask, sticking my brows up and giving her some sass. Michelle rolls her eyes and nods.

They won't miss me, I figure, as I stroll down the narrow hall and consider making a break for it. It's getting late, and before long Cameron will be over-tired and suggest a game of charades. Holly will go along with it because she worships the ground he walks on. And Katia will act cool and aloof but secretly plan to kick everyone's butts and win the game 10-1. Jonah will shamelessly flirt with Michelle all evening, and Ryder will make sarcastic comments from the corner while tapping away on his laptop.

I could totally sneak out the back door and make it home before anyone notices. The idea is tempting. All I have to do is text Michelle; tell her I'm sick, and that I have to go to bed.

Which is *kind of* true, because I'm sick of these lame parties.

I march to the back door and reach for it just as a face pops up to the glass. The sight of it makes me shriek so loud, a stampede of footsteps rushes towards me.

"What is it?" Holly cries, as the kitchen becomes crowded. I clamp my teeth together as the door swings open and the last person I want to bump into towers over me.

Perfect. Just when I think this night can't get any more awkward. *He's* here.

"Hey there Debbie. Did my manly muscles scare you? Sorry about that." His casual smirk tells me he's anything *but* sorry.

Typical Mark.

The room relaxes as everyone realizes I'm not being attacked.

"You're just in time, come on in and grab a drink," Michelle says as she bounces on the balls of her feet and her eyes glint at me.

Oh no. She's giving me that look. The one that tells me she's going to force me to do something I will absolutely regret in the morning.

Like the time she convinced me that climbing into her neighbor's hot tub was a good idea. She had *promised* me they were on vacation, and I guess that was true. But what she didn't know was their elderly parents were housesitting. We gave them the shock of their lives at 3am, when all of the liquor Michelle had had took over and she started singing *We Are the Champions* with all of the strength in her lungs.

Everyone files back into the living room and I follow, chewing my lip and swallowing the groan in my throat.

Mark settles on the couch, resting his ankle over his left knee and reclining back like he's the most chilled-out person in the room. Actually, he probably *is*. And yet, just the sight of him so confident and comfortable gets under my skin.

"Who's ready for a game?" Michelle asks. Everyone settles in their seats, except for Ryder who remains at the dining table with his laptop. His laser focus on the screen prompts me to think he's under the impression that if he doesn't make eye contact, he is invisible.

It works, no one so much as *looks* in his direction. My stomach knots with jealousy. I wish I could sit in the corner and get away with it.

"Everyone sit in a circle," Michelle barks. I look back to see her brandishing an empty bottle and a jar.

"Aren't we a bit old to be playing spin the bottle?" I ask with a brow raised. Katia stifles a giggle and grins over at me. I take it back. Maybe some of us aren't too mature for spin the bottle. Holly cosies up to Cameron and playfully strokes his back. He just scrolls through his phone, as if oblivious to the attention.

"We're not playing spin the bottle," Michelle says with a chuckle. As if I've just suggested we take a trip to the moon. That's right, silly Debbie with her wild ideas.

"Come on gorgeous, you can sit next to me." Mark pats the empty floor beside him and flashes me a smile. His heavy brows pinch together and he's smoldering. It's a look that would melt a thousand hearts. I imagine he's spent his entire life practicing in front of the mirror.

I give an exaggerated sigh and sit with my legs crossed. Katia's eyes shoot to Mark and return to my gaze as she gives me a knowing look. I keep eye contact and purse my lips. Yes, twin telepathy is totally a thing. I know that she's teasing me about Mark being my lover boy, or something. And I know she can read my warning.

Don't you dare say anything.

There are three people in this room that know a secret. But if Katia opens her mouth and lets the cat out of the bag, then I'm going to need to move state and change my name. It's embarrassing enough I have to face *him* again. But if Michelle, or Holly, or the guys knew about what happened at the lake last summer... I'd straight up die.

"So, what's the game?" I ask, breaking eye contact and looking at Michelle. She clears her throat and casts her eyes about us like we're a group of teenagers.

"Truth or Dare," she announces with a glint in her eyes.

Katia and I share a look. I guess Michelle thinks we are a group of teenagers. I can't even remember the last time I played *Truth or Dare*.

There's a grumble among the rest of the people sitting on the floor. To my surprise, Ryder settles next to Michelle and finally appears to show some interest. I never knew him to be the type to play childish games. Yet, neither am I, and look where we are.

"We spin the bottle to find out who goes first. These dares are designed to change your life."

"Why am I getting horror vibes from this? Nothing good ever came from a Truth or Dare game you know," Mark says. For the first time, I agree with his statement.

What if I have to tell everyone what happened between us last summer? I make a mental note to pick a dare. *Nothing* can be worse than sharing that.

"Hey, I just got my bachelor's in psychology. Trust me," Michelle says with her hands on her hips. It takes all of my resolve not to roll my eyes. "I've put a lot of thought into these challenges. And I promise, you're going to love them."

I glance at the sea of unimpressed looks in the room and my duty to support my bestie rises within me.

"Come on guys, it's Michelle's birthday. Let's just give it a go, shall we?" I offer, trying my best to impersonate a cheerleader and failing miserably. I worry my pitiful attempts to pump my arms and put on a smile makes me come across as sarcastic.

Despite my worries, everyone agrees.

"Great. Let's see who goes first," Michelle places the bottle on the carpet and sets it into a spin.

My stomach knots each time it faces me, and I chew my lip while keeping my eyes on the bottle.

Please don't land on me. Please don't land on me.

The bottle slows right near my knee and my heartrate quickens. Then, it stops.

"Mark, that's you," Michelle says brightly.

Cameron nudges Mark, who smirks.

"So Mark, truth or dare?" Michelle asks.

"Easy one. Dare," he says with confidence. I exhale, relieved he didn't pick truth. At least my secret is safe, for now. I wonder what dare could be so life-changing for Mark. Maybe he'll have to play chess against Ryder. And lose. Then he'll have to admit he's not *all that*.

The guy's ego is so inflated, it's a wonder how he can walk through doorways with such a big head.

"You need a partner to join this dare," Michelle says, looking at the piece of paper she picked out from the jar.

Mark's eyes shoot to mine and I want to kick him in the shin for even considering it.

Don't you dare.

"I'll choose Debbie," he says, his voice dripping with total satisfaction. My mouth hangs open. I stare at him wide-eyed, as the room erupts into laughter, then I shoot Michelle a look. Her eyes wrinkle at the corners as her face breaks into the evilest grin.

"Perfect," she said.

—Binge the whole series, free in Kindle Unlimited here:

What I Don't Like About You

Printed in Great Britain
by Amazon

76084857R00108